"Yesss," Luke hi[ss...] and forth, her soft hair beneath his fingers. *"Yes, yes, yes."*

Callie worked her magic, with her fingers, her tongue leading him into uncharted territory. She gently guided him to a paradise he'd only dreamed of.

But this wasn't a dream. The warm wetness of her mouth, the sweet taste of her kiss still lingering, the heavenly smell of her, the sound of the ocean wafting through the open bedroom doors. This new awareness of him, or her, was breaking up his brittle outer shell.

She was beyond beauty to Luke. Callie was pure life, pure joy. She and her sensual impulses merged together against all the rules of proper conduct. Her mouth moved over him without caution or fear. She pushed him past his knowledge of himself. He had never before been so physically possessed. Her movements shook his world. The walls of the hotel room seemed to ripple. Could this be an earthquake?

No. There was no tremor in the ground, only his body.

Luke was nervous and exalted and awed. And he accepted the inevitable....

Dear Reader,

Ever since I started writing for Harlequin Blaze line I've wanted to create a story about a sexually inexperienced man schooled by a woman well versed in the erotic arts. I knew he would have to be a special guy: honorable, full of integrity, a little straitlaced but open to experimentation. And thus bodyguard Luke Cardasian was born. He's Sir Galahad and the Lone Ranger rolled into one.

But he needed a woman who could excavate his long-suppressed passion. A bold and daring radio shock jock like Callie Ryder. A woman who's not afraid of expressing her sexuality.

Writing *Shockingly Sensual* was not only lots of fun, but it was also challenging trying to figure out how Callie was going to coax Luke into breaking all his own rules. I'd love to hear what you think about the story. You can visit me on the Web at www.loriwilde.com or write to me at Lori Wilde, P.O. Box 31, Weatherford, TX 76085.

Enjoy!

Lori Wilde

Books by Lori Wilde

HARLEQUIN BLAZE

Don't miss any of our special offers. Write to us at the following address for information on our newest releases.

Harlequin Reader Service
U.S.: 3010 Walden Ave., P.O. Box 1325, Buffalo, NY 14269
Canadian: P.O. Box 609, Fort Erie, Ont. L2A 5X3

SHOCKINGLY SENSUAL

Lori Wilde

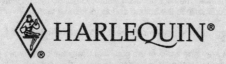

HARLEQUIN®

TORONTO • NEW YORK • LONDON
AMSTERDAM • PARIS • SYDNEY • HAMBURG
STOCKHOLM • ATHENS • TOKYO • MILAN • MADRID
PRAGUE • WARSAW • BUDAPEST • AUCKLAND

To hardworking moms everywhere. If my books can
provide you with a small respite from your hectic day
I am truly honored. Thank you so much for reading.

ISBN 0-373-79179-8

SHOCKINGLY SENSUAL

Copyright © 2005 by Laurie Vanzura.

www.eHarlequin.com

Printed in U.S.A.

1

"HEY DAWGS…how y'all doin'? This is KSXX comin' to you live from the heart of Manhattan. I'm Callie Ryder, your late-night host for all things hot and sensual." The woman's smoky amber voice oozed pure honey from the Bose stereo speakers in the black leather dashboard.

Luke Cardasian sat in the passenger seat of the Humvee that his older brother, Zack, had just purchased for their family-owned security firm. Restlessly, he drummed his fingers against the armrest, breathing in the new car smell. Luke didn't approve of his brother's extravagant expenditure, but he had to admit, the Hummer made quite a statement. Rather guiltily, he admired the way the powerful vehicle made him feel.

Strong, in control, invincible.

"Tonight," whispered the lady deejay, "we're discussing hard-ons."

What?

Startled, Luke stared at the radio. He was convinced that he must have heard the woman incorrectly.

"How to get 'em, how to keep 'em, and what to do with them once you've got 'em. Come on my radio, peeps, pick up those telephones and call me. Let's talk erections."

Let's talk erections?

"What's that garbage you're listening to," he growled at Zack.

Luke had been out of the country for the last six years guiding aid workers and journalists through the war-torn country of Limbasa, where he'd spent much of his childhood. And even before he'd gone to Limbasa, he'd been in the navy for four years and stationed at various ports of call around the world. He hadn't lived in the U.S. for any extended length of time since he was eighteen and he'd forgotten exactly how liberated the American media could be. Talk about culture shock.

He'd returned home—just as the war in Limbasa was winding to a close—to help Zack run the family business after a heart attack had forced their father into early retirement and that's exactly what he was going to do. No matter how much trouble he was having adjusting.

"Get out. You've never heard the Midnight Ryder?" Zack asked.

"How could I?' he said. "I've only been home three days."

Zack tisked his tongue. "You've been away too long, bro. Here's my recommendation if you want to shake the Limbasa desert off your feet and get back into the swing of things. Let your hair grow out of that buzz cut, start paying attention to what's popular and, for crying out loud, buy some new clothes."

"What's wrong with the way I'm dressed?" Luke glanced down at his black T-shirt, green camouflage pants and black leather combat boots. His clothes said he meant business. "We *are* running a security firm."

"And the clients want a bodyguard, not a guerilla freedom fighter. You look like you're armed for hand-to-hand combat with the modern world."

"Maybe it's the other way around," Luke muttered defensively. "And it's the modern world that's armed for combat with me. Women are talking about erections on the radio for crying out loud."

"And that's bad because…?"

"It's just not in good taste."

Zack shook his head. "Face facts, you're too damned rigid for your own good. Loosen up on the principles, will ya? For the sake of our clients, if not for me."

It wasn't the first time they'd had this disagreement. He and his brother were opposites in almost every way. Luke was serious, reliable and self-disciplined. Whereas easily swayed Zack could always see both sides of an issue, and he often relied on a joke or a quick smile to get himself out of trouble.

They had both been born in the United States but when Zack was six and Luke was four, their father, a former military attaché, had been sent to Limbasa. They had lived there for ten years until Dad's career brought the family stateside again. When Luke was in high school, his father had retired from the military and started his own security business in Manhattan.

Like their father, Luke placed a high value on both honor and idealism. That was why the navy had been such a perfect fit for him. Then later, when Mukasi Umbasi, a childhood friend of his from Limbasa, had called with the horror stories about starvation and land mines and other war atrocities, Luke knew he had to return to the country where he'd spent so much of his life and help out those kind, loving people any way he could.

Zack was more like their peacemaking mother, who saw the best in everyone whether they deserved her generosity or not. And while Luke admired his older brother's ability to take life as he found it, he was worried they would clash in their approach to business. Luke already felt Zack was profligate, as evidenced by the purchase of the Humvee. Zack on the other hand had accused Luke of being tightfisted and having no zest for life.

He had plenty of zest. He just didn't go crazy buying stuff he didn't really need.

"How can one possibly be *too* principled?" Luke asked.

"By expecting everyone else to live up to your unrealistic standards. We're not all like you," Zack said. "Nor do we want to be."

Luke let the comment slide. He had other things to think about. Like his first bodyguard assignment that he was starting that evening.

Zack hadn't given him many details about the job. All Luke knew was that he'd be guarding an author on her book tour. Apparently, the writer had been receiving disturbing stalker-type mail from a disgruntled fan and her business manager had hired Cardasian Personal Security Services as a prophylactic measure.

So here they were, on their way to meet the author because Luke had wanted to get a feel for the woman's security needs before leaving tomorrow on their flight to Los Angeles. Zack had told him that the writer was an insomniac who worked offbeat hours and that was why they were meeting her so late. Her night owl habits suited Luke just fine. He often had difficulty sleeping as well.

Ah yes. Work.

This was exactly what he needed to keep his mind off the fact that he hadn't had sex in more years than he cared to count. A job, an assignment, something to focus his attention on.

As they drove through Times Square, Luke glanced up to see a photograph of a slender young woman with short, spiky, fire-engine-red hair poised high above the traffic. She was dressed in a black leather miniskirt, see-through black lace blouse, thigh-high, four-inch-heeled black vinyl boots and lots of silver jewelry. Her bright, intelligent eyes were ringed with far too much black eye shadow and her slick wet lips were as red as her hair.

And Luke could not pry his gaze away from her as the Hummer idled at the stoplight. She exuded a raw sexuality that leaped right off the billboard. In the picture she was seated on a stool in front of a microphone, her legs spread wide and three fingers splayed across her open mouth. The coy expression on her gamine face suggested that she'd just blurted out something scandalous.

While she was pretending wide-eyed shock at her own audacious statement, you could tell by the naughty twinkle in her chocolate-brown eyes that she was anything but remorseful.

The bold lettering above her head declared: Callie Ryder Gives Shockingly Good Sex.

This then was the woman from the radio talk show.

In his opinion, the sign was in appalling taste. They

were overexposing Callie's assets and hinting that she was a wanton woman. He supposed that was the point. Stir up controversy, lure in listeners.

What bothered him the most, however, was his body's immediate and rather forceful response to the manipulative advertisement. His gut clenched, his pulse rate accelerated and he felt a hard pressure build inside him. He must be in bad shape, lusting after a woman on a billboard.

What in the hell was the matter with him? Why was he so turned on? She was nothing more than a superficial Madison Avenue image and the exact opposite of the type of woman he was normally attracted to. Luke preferred sweet-natured, full-figured brunettes, not scrappy, ultrathin women whose hair color did not even occur in nature.

"Now she's some kind of firecracker," Zack commented, gazing up at the billboard for so long the driver in the vehicle behind them leaned hard on the car horn.

"Don't you have a fiancée?" Luke asked, sneaking one last look over his shoulder as they motored from Times Square.

"Hey, just because I'm getting married doesn't mean I'm dead. I can still appreciate talent." Zack grinned. "Besides, who do you think got me hooked on the Midnight Ryder?"

"Belinda likes this junk?"

"Just listen." Zack dialed up the volume. Luke rolled his eyes.

"Hello, Gina from Queens," Callie greeted her caller. "What's *up* in your life?"

"It's about my boyfriend, but…it's kinda embarrassing." The woman's sharp New York accent clashed in dramatic contrast to Callie's languid, Southern drawl.

"Honey," Callie murmured, "it's just sex. Let's talk about it."

Just sex?

Luke shook his head. Call him old-fashioned, but he had never understood how so many people could take sex so lightly. Intimacy had consequences and you'd better be prepared to deal with them before you jumped into bed with a stranger, otherwise you could end up getting hurt.

Big-time.

"Does your boyfriend have trouble achieving an erection?" Callie asked.

"Nooo," Gina said.

"He just doesn't last long, is that it?"

"Uh…er…well," Gina stammered. "I don't really know."

"How can you not know?"

"He's twenty-five and he's never been with a woman and he's afraid to…um…you know…have sex with me."

"And why is your boyfriend afraid?" Callie murmured to Gina from Queens in a sexy tone that sent unexpected tingles slithering straight up Luke's spine.

"Well, I'm the experienced one and he's scared he won't be able to please me like my previous lovers," Gina replied.

"Do you have the same fears?"

"Yeah." Gina hesitated. "Kinda…so what can we do to get over this hump?"

"You mean besides humping?" Callie teased.

Luke winced but Gina laughed. "I really like the guy, but I'm about ready to call it quits. We've been dating for over two months and we're no closer to having sex than we were on the first date. My friends think there's something wrong with him if he's a twenty-five-year-old virgin. They want me to dump him."

"No, no, Gina," Callie said. Luke heard the excitement in her voice escalating as she spoke, and it corresponded with his own arousal. "I think it's really sort of sweet that your boyfriend has waited until he's emotionally ready before diving into sex. More men should be so self-aware. You don't seem to realize what a terrific prospect you have on your hands."

Luke arched an eyebrow. He was surprised that a woman who spoke so frankly about intimate sexual matters hadn't immediately condemned the poor sap for not having been born an accomplished lover. Grudgingly he adjusted his estimation of Callie Ryder. But just by an inch, which still put her a rung below door-to-door salesmen.

"Whadda ya mean?" Gina asked suspiciously. "I don't understand."

"You have a golden opportunity to teach your guy how *you* like to be pleasured," Callie explained. "He's a clean slate. He has no bad habits to break. No expectations to shatter."

"Hmm. That is true. I never thought about it that way."

"Next time you're making out, take his hand in yours and use his fingers to trace a road map over your body. Linger where you want him to linger. Skim where you want him to skim. Show that man exactly how to trip your trigger."

Even though he was trying not to let Callie's sultry tone suck him in, Luke couldn't deny the heated rush of sensation filling him as he imagined tracing his hand over *her* erogenous zones.

"But won't me taking charge like that make him feel, uh…well, emasculated?"

"Which is worse? Your boyfriend feeling emasculated or you feeling horny?"

Gina giggled.

"Seriously, all joking aside," Callie continued, "you'll need to proceed with tender consideration and kindness."

"Please, tell me how?"

"Don't be demanding or judgmental of his current technique. He is doing the best he knows how and men do tend to have delicate egos when it comes to their prowess in bed. Light a few candles, dress up in a naughty outfit, slip on some sexy music and lead him where you want him to go."

"But I'm not so sure I can be that bold. I'm not you, Callie."

"Of course you can. Make a role-playing game of it. Indulge your secret fantasies."

"Like how?" Gina asked.

"Imagine if you will a beautiful courtesan. She's intelligent, elegant and dynamite in bed. She could have her pick of any number of powerful men who lust after her, but they only care about sating their own needs. What our hungry courtesan yearns for is a man who quakes at the very thought of fulfilling her every sensuous desire." Callie spun her web, luring listeners into her erotic world with whiskey-voiced cheekiness. Clearly the woman was enjoying her own tale.

"Our courtesan loves to be in control. So she eschews the older lovers who long to possess her because she is a woman who refuses to be owned. Instead, she favors the strapping young stable man who works in the livery."

Luke moistened his lips which had gone suddenly dry.

"She likes how he blushes whenever she says something shocking," Callie went on. "She appreciates the way his dark serious eyes follow her as she mounts her unruly stallion. She particularly enjoys his rich, masculine scent."

Luke felt his body blaze hot in all the right places as this X-rated Scheherazade swept him away. If he were home alone right now he would doubtlessly be taking matters into his own hand. He stifled a groan, irritated because he was so darned susceptible.

He disapproved of her bawdy talk show at the very same time he was inexplicably drawn to her outrageousness. He wished he could be so imaginative, so spontaneous, so free.

But how did a guy learn to go against his very nature?

Zack nudged him in the ribs with his elbow. "Didn't I tell you she was good?"

"The courtesan decides she must have this naive young man as her lover," Callie murmured. "In the dead of night, she puts on a sexy crimson dressing gown made of the finest satin and slips off to the stables bent on seducing him."

The sound engineer in the control room cued suggestive *boom-shaka-boom-shaka-boom* music to accompany Callie's titillating tale.

"Our courtesan finds the stable man stripped naked to the waist, tossing fresh hay into the horse stalls. He takes one long look at her and his eyes widen with nervousness as his manhood hardens with pure, unadulterated lust. He knows this is wrong, but he can't stop his body's reaction."

Boom-shaka-boom-shaka-boom.

Luke squirmed. Too much. Too much. Too much. Unnerved, he ached to reach over and snap off the radio, but his fingers refused to unfurl themselves from the clenched fists resting solidly against his tensed thighs.

He was in that barn.

He was that weak-kneed liveryman, and in his mind, the saucy courtesan was none other than the shocking Callie Ryder.

His blood pumped in his ears, pumped through his veins, pumped, pumped in his groin.

Pump, pump, pump.

"She steps across the wooden floor."

Creaking noises issued from the sound engineer's mixing board. Creak, creak, creak.

"And she reaches out to trace her fingers over the lines and planes of his hard, sweaty chest. The room smells of leather and man and hay and horses," Callie said huskily. "Her bosom heaves. Her blood is boiling. Her passion erupting with stark, feral need."

Luke could see the entire scene as sharply as if he were watching a film. Startled, he realized Callie was getting off on the fantasy of mentoring an inexperienced lover, just as he was getting off on the idea of being tutored by a lusty, knowledgeable woman.

"And then they are making love, tearing off each other's clothes. Making, molding, melting, squeezing, slapping, sucking life into their bodies. Feeling the richness of their souls as they become one. Joined, melded, fused." Callie was almost panting as she breathed the final word.

Sweet, sweet, sweet.

He visualized it all. The courtesan, the stable man. She was her and he was him and they were in a sweaty tangle of arms and legs and lips and skin.

Luke gulped, battling back his arousal. *Stop thinking about sex!*

But he could not.

The more he tried to stop, the clearer he saw her. Her firm high breasts, her luscious lips, her long lean legs.

Luke clamped his mouth closed and shifted uncomfortably. The caller from Queens could have been speaking about him. While he wasn't a virgin, he wasn't exactly notching bedposts, either. He'd been so focused on his work in Limbasa there had never been much time or opportunity for romance.

Even when he'd taken R and R in Italy and Switzerland, Luke had avoided sexual encounters. He knew it wouldn't have been fair to either himself or a potential partner to get involved in a long-distance relationship. And he had simply never been the kind of guy who went in for sex whenever and wherever. He just didn't see the point.

So he'd waited.

And waited.

Maybe a lot of men wouldn't understand his patience, but Luke had always sensed that when the right woman came along, he would know it.

Turning his head, he stared out the window at the crush of heavy foot traffic and faked like he wasn't listening to the radio program. Having grown up in two distinctly different countries, he never felt as if he belonged to either one. Too liberated for Limbasa, too inhibited for America. For most of his life he'd felt as if he was on the outside looking in. A misfit.

It was eleven-thirty on a Friday night and Broadway was awash in an eclectic assortment of people. From well-dressed theatergoers trying to grab a taxi. To the hip young party crowd on the prowl. To swing-shift workers hitting the clubs for a nightcap before going home. The city throbbed with energy.

But it was a different kind of energy than Luke was used to and nothing was making that clearer than the sassy female deejay.

In desperation, he scanned the crowd on the street again, searching for something, anything to derail his irrational train of thought. His military preparation had given him an acute eye for detail. He noticed things most people would miss. In the throng, he spotted a woman as she exited a bar. She had her purse slung casually over her shoulder. The clasp was not secured and it flapped open with each step she took.

A lanky teen with bad skin pushed away from the side of the building where he'd been leaning and loped after her.

The kid is going to steal her purse.

The thought ran through Luke's head and he didn't question it. Life in Limbasa had taught him to trust his gut instincts. His intuition had saved the day on more than one occasion.

"Pull over," he told Zack.

"What?"

"That punk is about to steal a woman's purse, but he's not going to get away with it," Luke said, unbuckling his seat belt and yanking open the Humvee's door before Zack had even come to a complete stop.

"Luke, that's no…"

But he didn't hear the rest of his brother's sentence because the teen had made his move, planting a palm against the woman's back and shoving her to the ground at the same moment he snatched the handbag.

The kid sprinted to the corner just as Luke's feet hit the pavement. In four long-legged strides, he caught up with him. He slapped a hand at the kid's collar, fisted the material of his shirt and jerked him backward and up off his feet.

"Now, now," he growled, low and deadly. His bicep bulged as he held the struggling teen aloft. "That's not very nice. Stealing a lady's purse."

The kid made sputtering noises. "Lemme go, you butthead."

Luke held out his other hand. "First, fork over the purse."

"Go steal your own. This one's mine," the defiant kid said, even though his face was turning red from the pressure Luke applied to his collar.

Not wanting to actually harm the kid, Luke lowered him to the ground, clamped his other hand around his wrist before he let go of his collar and then wrenched the handbag away from him.

"Hey, hey, what are you doin'?" the kid protested as Luke started dragging him back down the street. "Get your hands off me."

"You're going to apologize," Luke said through clenched teeth. Being held responsible for his actions was the only way the teenager was going to learn to respect others.

"I ain't apologizing for nothin'."

"Would you rather I called the police?"

The kid just scowled.

The crowd stared. Luke searched for the woman who'd lost her purse and caught sight of her.

She rushed forward and in a dark, gravelly voice said breathlessly, "You got my purse back for me, you big ol' hunk of manhood."

Now that she was standing just a few feet away, Luke was disconcerted to realize that she was no woman. Her features were decidedly masculine. Large nose, iron jaw, false eyelashes, no breasts.

Aw hell. He had just rescued a cross-dresser in distress.

Luke was so unnerved he let go of the kid, who immediately sprinted off down a side street.

"My hero." The cross-dresser accepted the purse Luke thrust at him. The guy clutched his hammy palms together in a dramatic gesture and batted his faux eyelashes suggestively. "Can I buy you a drink to express my appreciation?"

"No thanks." Luke grunted, pivoted on his heel and stalked away.

Desperate to escape, he glanced around for the Humvee and spotted Zack double-parked with the engine running, laughing his ass off.

"I tried to tell you that was no lady," Zack said, once Luke had slammed the door closed behind him. "But you're always judging a book by its cover."

"You're enjoying this, aren't you?" Luke glowered darkly.

"Yep."

"It doesn't matter," he muttered. "She or he, whatever the case may be, did not deserve to have money stolen by some badly reared kid."

Zack shook his head. "The Lone Ranger galloping to the rescue."

"Shut up and drive before you get ticketed for parking in a tow-away zone."

A hot flush of embarrassment spread up the back of Luke's neck. He felt like an idiot. Was he actually so naive that he'd been unable to distinguish the difference between a real woman and a man in drag?

Apparently so. Luke winced. Okay, maybe Zack was right. He was experiencing culture shock. Time to get his mind back where it belonged. On the job at hand.

"So," Luke said, "forget about the distractions and tell me more about this assignment. What's the client's name?"

Still chuckling, Zack nodded at the glove compartment. "File's in there."

Luke opened the glove compartment and took out a

brown file folder. He unhooked the clasp, slid the papers out and was confused to find himself staring at Callie Ryder's head shot.

"I don't understand." He frowned. "What's this about?"

"The client in question."

"Excuse me?"

"Our gal Callie has written a book about her adventures as a female shock jock. That was why I tuned the radio in to her program. Give you a sneak preview of what you're in for." Zack's grin was wicked.

"You mean she's the one I'll be guarding?" His stomach plummeted to the bottom of his combat boots.

"Yep."

"You're enjoying making me uncomfortable about this," he accused.

"Kinda, yeah." Zack winked. "Just think, you and Callie alone together."

"On the road," Luke muttered, his dread growing by the minute.

"Close quarters," Zack confirmed.

"For three weeks?"

"That's right. Think of it as a vacation. When we were kids you would lighten up considerably when we went on trips. Just remember what they say in show biz. What happens on the road stays on the road. If you get my drift."

Luke got it all right. He was stuck riding herd over the sexiest woman he had never wanted to meet, on a cross-country road trip for the next twenty-one days with a raging libido and a moral code that would not allow him to act on his baser impulses no matter how much he might want to.

Great. Just great.

"Dream come true, huh?" Zack laughed.

Dream, hell, more like his worst nightmare.

2

"WE'LL BE RIGHT BACK following the news at the midnight hour," Callie purred seductively. "Give me a call so we can continue our scintillating discussion about hard-ons. Come on, New York, let's talk about sex."

The 'on-air' light flashed off in the control booth at the KSXX studios as the program engineer, Barb Johnson, cut to the pretaped news. Callie removed her headset, took a long sip of bottled water to wet her dry mouth and then plowed a hand through her short, spiky hair recently dyed flamboyant fuchsia. Her jaunty, carefree movements sent the numerous sterling-silver bracelets at her wrist jangling merrily.

"Whew, Cal, that virgin livery guy fantasy was a hot one." Barb fanned herself. "I need a freezing cold shower and for once it's not from menopause."

To be honest, the brazen courtesan scenario had gotten Callie pretty revved up, too. Her own hottest secret sex dreams always revolved around seducing an inexperienced, but exceptionally willing man and single-handedly schooling him into becoming the best lover on the planet.

In fact, she had a distinct mental picture of this raw,

diamond-in-the-rough fantasy lover. He would be tall and very masculine. Dark hair, dark eyes, broad shoulders, washboard abs. He would have a powerful, commanding presence while at the same time possessing tender inner sensibilities.

A strapping manly man who also had a nurturing, caring side.

She had in mind a modern day Sir Galahad. Chaste and pure of heart and loyal to a fault and with amazing self-control.

And she would be the one who corrupted him.

Gooseflesh spread up her arms and she licked her lips as she vividly imagined her hero. Ready, willing and anxious to please.

Her lover would have a dormant lustiness just waiting to be exposed by her. He would show his gratitude for her generosity by giving her the most incredible orgasms of her life.

And as she lay trembling and sated in his arms, he would scoop her up and take her to a steaming bubble bath where he would gently bathe her and then shampoo her hair. He would paint her toenails and give her a massage and then he would make love to her all over again.

Callie gulped. She could see him as clearly as if he was a real person.

She was not sure why this particular scenario appealed to her so much. Maybe it was because she liked being in charge, or perhaps it was because she longed to be pampered by a fervent partner.

Either way, the fantasy popped up in her dreams with alarming regularity. Tonight, her caller from Queens had given Callie carte blanche to explore her most furtive desires on the air.

And explore she had.

What a lark!

She had learned a long time ago if she could turn herself on, she could turn her listeners on. And boy was she turned on. Ergo, her listeners must be going at it like bunnies. Her body was still tingling from the heady hormonal rush. She just hoped she didn't end up with a hefty fine from the FCC for crossing the line from intriguing to indecent.

"I'm gonna give Thaddeus a call, tell him to be up and ready when I get home," Barb said, referring to her husband of twenty-five years. "I am in the mood for some lovin'."

Barb was a forty-something, cocoa-skinned beauty impeccably dressed in a feminine pale pink pantsuit that contrasted radically with Callie's bold green camouflage-colored micromini, black halter top and lace-up combat boots.

"I'm glad you liked the program." Callie grinned. "And I hope Thaddeus appreciates the fallout."

"I'm sure he will." Barb winked. "How do you keep coming up with these fascinating fantasies night after night?"

"Guess I'm just lucky I have a dirty mind." She chuckled.

"Lucky, hell. You're damned talented."

"You flatter me," Callie said.

"Please." Barb snorted. "Why do you think *Let's Talk About Sex* just got picked up in the West Coast market?

The phone lines are jammed. We've had over six hundred calls and this is a Wednesday night. Everyone wants the ear of the Midnight Ryder. And his Highness would kill for numbers like that." She grinned and jerked a thumb at the poster on the wall above her head.

"You think?"

"I know," Barb said.

Callie leaned back in her chair and eyed the glossy advertisement poster depicting the reigning king of KSXX talk radio, Buck Bryson.

Buck was well into middle age but tried to diminish his years by wearing his hair too long and hiding behind a pair of pricey designer sunglasses. He was a master at his job and Callie had studied his techniques. She owed the senior deejay a lot, whether Buck realized it or not.

"You've got old Bucky boy on the ropes, babe," Barb said. "Did you hear? He has taken to making snide comments about you on the morning show."

"Buck's bad-mouthing me? I would say that is a very good sign."

"J-e-a-l-o-u-s." Barb spelled out the word. "The man is running scared."

"You exaggerate." Callie smiled modestly.

"Like hell. One day in the very near future I predict his slot will be yours if you want it."

Callie didn't lust after the morning slot because she would have to tone down her format to comply with the more restricted a.m. regulations and of course she'd be forced to change her handle. How could the Midnight Ryder be on at 6 a.m?

She didn't even crave the big bump in pay that went

with the morning slot. She was competitive only to the degree that a better time slot got her more exposure and more exposure helped her get her message out to more women.

Sex is fun. Dive right in and make no excuses for enjoying yourself.

Callie believed the world was full of sexy, exciting possibilities and it was her mission to spread the word via her talk show. Her lusty outlook on life came from having a forward-thinking, feminist mom who had sat her down when she was nine and told her everything she needed to know about sex. Including a protracted contraceptive demonstration that had concluded with her mother rolling a condom onto an unpeeled banana.

Mom had topped off the talk by handing her a catalogue of sex toys and then giving her this bizarre advice: "Remember, Cal gal, a woman needs a man like a trout needs a Harley."

Callie still wasn't sure what that meant but she had learned to appreciate and revel in her sensuality without feeling the least bit guilty. If Buck had understood that Callie was driven solely by the desire to help other women find their own inner sex goddess, he probably wouldn't have felt so obligated to bad-mouth her.

Callie got to her feet just as her business manager and longtime friend, Molly Anne Armstrong, appeared on the opposite side of the soundproof glass booth. She was clutching a manila folder and crooking an index finger at her.

Even at midnight in a nearly empty radio station, Molly Anne was dressed in a professional navy pin-striped suit, sensible flats and her ubiquitous tortoiseshell spectacles. Molly Anne had twenty-twenty visual acuity. She just wore the glasses because she thought they made her look more intelligent.

"The proper image," Molly Anne was fond of saying, "is everything."

Callie and Molly Anne had grown up together in the same rough neighborhood in Winslow, Georgia, not far from the hospital where their single mothers had worked as emergency-room nurses on the graveyard shift. They had been latchkey kids, eating far more than their share of sugary breakfast cereals and frozen TV dinners and microwave popcorn.

When they were sixteen—after Callie caught her boyfriend cheating on her, and Molly Anne got stood up for the junior prom—they had made a pact to never trust men. And they had sealed their sworn oath by pricking their fingers with a medical lancet they'd swiped from Callie's mom's first-aid kit. Signing their names in blood, they vowed never to let a guy come between them.

The pact had held up for eighteen years.

During that time Molly Anne had been there for Callie's smart-mouthed antics, which began as nothing more than a defense mechanism. Callie rebelled against a father who had no time for her once he'd divorced her mother, married a much younger wife just eight years older than Callie and had a cute little baby daughter of their own.

Callie had been summarily replaced.

The teenage Callie had relished the attention her naughty behavior attracted. Particularly when her outrageousness landed her into hot water with authority figures and forced her father away from his precious new family.

But secretly she had never felt quite as bold as she pretended to be. Now, her audacious persona earned her boatloads of money and legions of hip young fans. Yet she occasionally felt trapped by her guise. Being New York City's premiere female shock jock was getting a little claustrophobic and she often found herself wondering what might have been if she'd chosen an alternative path.

Callie stepped into the hallway, closing the door softly behind her. "What's up, Moll?"

"We've received another one." Molly Anne was worrying her bottom lip with her top teeth and not meeting Callie's gaze.

In spite of their long relationship, upbeat Callie had never quite gotten used to Molly Anne's the-sky-is-perpetually-falling outlook on life. Sometimes her business manager's wet-blanket attitude irked Callie so much she wondered why they had remained friends for as long as they had.

Probably because worrywart Molly Anne balanced out Callie's gung-ho approach.

And there was that pact.

"Another what?" Callie asked.

Molly Anne waved the now familiar gold and green envelope under Callie's nose. "You were wrong about this guy. He's escalating his threats."

For the past few months, KSXX had been receiving ranting letters about *Let's Talk About Sex* from an anonymous disgruntled listener. The guy blamed Callie for everything from the breakup of his marriage, to the degeneration of the country's collective morality, to the recent jump in fuel prices.

She figured the dude was just an uptight crackpot with a couple of loose screws and an axe to grind. She really hadn't given him much credence. As long as her ratings were high and the station didn't mind a little controversy, why should she?

"I'm sure the guy is basically harmless." Callie shrugged.

"He's not harmless," Molly Anne said. "This time he's threatened your life."

"Let me see that." Callie snatched the envelope from Molly Anne's hand. It was a typewritten letter addressed to the station manager, Roger McKee.

Since KSXX has repeatedly ignored my request to remove the recalcitrant Ms. Ryder's offensive program from the airwaves, you've left me no choice but to take matters into my own hands. One way or the other, I'm determined to silence her from polluting young minds with her lax moral values. If she mysteriously disappears during her upcoming book tour, then you'll have only yourselves to blame for her demise.

As always, the letter was unsigned.

"He knows about your book tour," Molly Anne emphasized.

"It's no secret. We've been pitching the tour during sign-off every night for the past two months."

"Yes, but he's threatening you while you're on the book tour."

"Okay," Callie said. "So the guy is a certifiable whack job. That doesn't mean he's really going to try and snuff me."

"Roger called the police and they're trying to run down who sent the letter. In the meantime, the cops advised that we hire our own protection for your book tour. So guess what?"

"What?" Callie eyed her suspiciously.

"You've got a bodyguard."

"You're not serious." Callie made a face like she'd bitten into a fresh lemon.

"The board of directors insists," Molly Anne said.

"Tell them I refused. I'll take full responsibility for my own safety. I'll sign a release form if it'll appease legal, but I'm not going to let some lunatic have me running scared."

"The company has a great deal invested in you, Callie. They're just protecting their interests. Don't fight them on this."

"Oh that gives me such a warm fuzzy feeling." She felt manipulated and she didn't care for the sensation. "I'm just a commodity to the powers that be."

"Just this once will you please act reasonably? Don't let your need to control everything override common sense," Molly Anne cautioned.

"I don't have a need to control everything."

"Ha."

"I don't," Callie denied and pouched out her bottom lip in a pout. "I just like doing things my own way."

"That's the definition of control."

"No it's not."

"Then prove you're not a control freak. Accept the bodyguard."

"But I can take care of myself," she argued. "Do I have to remind you that my mother sent me to self-defense classes for eight years? I've got more belts than Jackie Chan."

At that remark, Molly Anne whipped off her jacket and rolled up the sleeve of her white silk blouse to reveal a jagged scar running almost the length of her forearm. "And need I remind you about this? You're not as invincible as you think you are."

Remorsefully, she shook her head. Her friend had acquired the scar when Callie, after the sum total of eleven karate lessons, had insisted on standing up to a schoolyard bully when they were in sixth grade. Callie had actually managed to hold her own before the kid slammed her into Molly Anne. Her friend fell backward onto an exposed metal pipe.

It took thirty-four stitches to close the wound and Callie felt awful about Molly Anne getting hurt, but the results spoke for themselves. The bully had never bothered them again.

"Please, Callie, do this for me," Molly Anne pleaded. "Where would I be if something happened to you?"

"You would be fine."

Molly Anne wrapped her fingers around Callie's forearm and squeezed gently. "I don't even want to think about losing you."

"You're not going to lose me."

"You don't know that," Molly Anne said.

"Come on, don't you think you're blowing this whole thing out of proportion?"

"You might be right. But Roger's already hired the bodyguard," Molly Anne said.

"What? I can't believe you didn't tell me about this before now."

"I didn't tell you because I knew this is how you would react. But here's the deal and I'm afraid it's non-negotiable. If you don't agree to the bodyguard, KSXX will no longer underwrite your tour. Go it on your own and you can pick up the forty grand price tag."

"You're kidding," Callie said.

"I'm not."

"This totally sucks."

"Sorry." Molly Anne raised her palms.

"I'm being railroaded." Callie glared. After having just purchased an apartment in SoHo, she was in no position to shell out that kind of cash for her own book tour. "This is exactly what the creep wants. He gets off on terrorizing women."

Plus, the last thing she wanted was some stuffy, flat-footed bodyguard breathing down her neck for the next three weeks. She'd been looking forward to letting her professional facade slip a bit once she was out on the road, away from home turf.

Sure, she would have to be "on" for the book signings and the publicity events, but she harbored secret hopes that once she left the hustle and bustle of New York behind, she could finagle some alone time and do some serious thinking about the future.

And the past.

Because lately she'd been pining for the girl she'd buried deep down inside before she'd first donned the outrageous Midnight Ryder persona and things had changed forever.

It was exhausting, spending your life pretending to be something you really weren't. Although years of "fake it until you make it" ultimately had altered Callie's personality. But while her outlandish behavior had perched her on the verge of stardom, it was also slowly robbing her of her authenticity.

At twenty-eight she wasn't even sure who she was anymore.

"Cheer up," Molly Anne said. "He might be cute."

"He who?" Callie frowned.

"Your bodyguard. He's on his way over here to meet you as we speak."

"He's coming here?" she asked. "Tonight? But I have a show to finish."

"That's perfect. He can see you in action. Get an appreciation for what you do."

Callie started to protest but then the ingrained habit to shock took over and she grinned wickedly instead. "If he's cute maybe I'll do him."

"Callie!" That got a rise out of Molly Anne just as she'd intended.

"Well, if KSXX insists on forcing a bodyguard on me, I might as well make full use of him. Three weeks on the road, close quarters. If he's single, why not?"

"Because it's unethical for a bodyguard to have sex with the woman he's guarding."

"There's a bodyguard code of ethics?"

"I don't know," Molly Anne said, flustered. She got discombobulated so easily it was almost no fun yanking her chain. "But there oughta be."

Barb waved a hand at Callie, sending her the familiar "break is over" gesture and cueing up the intro song. Molly Anne scooted from the control room into the observation booth.

ZZ Top's "Tube Steak Boogie" segued from the commercial into the program's return. Callie reached for her headset as the "on air" light flashed.

"Ah, yes. Who among us can't appreciate a little tube steak boogie?" she asked.

"Callie," Barb interjected. "We have Dave from Albany on line one. Dave's problem is that he can't tame his hard-ons."

"Talk to me, Dave from Albany," Callie murmured. "I'm listening."

Silence.

In radio there was nothing worse than dead air. First, Callie thought the caller had hung up, but then she realized someone was breathing on the other end.

Oh swell. A pervert. Was it going to be that kind of night?

"Dave," she said. "Are you there?"

"You think you're hot stuff, dontcha?" the man snarled.

"Excuse me?"

Her hackles lifted. She fisted her hands and squared her shoulders, readying herself for a fight. In the observation booth Molly Anne was jumping up and down and making a slicing motion across her neck with an index finger.

But Callie would rather be dead than cowed. She shook her head at Barb. *Don't cut him off.*

She refused to allow this bozo to intimidate her. She'd learned never to back down from a tyrant.

"You heard me," he continued. "Every night you're showing off, preening for your listeners. It's because of you that my girlfriend left me. She claimed I didn't treat her like she deserved to be treated."

There was something vaguely familiar about his voice, but she couldn't place it. "Maybe your girlfriend had a point. Did you treat her badly, Dave?"

"Who in the hell do you think you are?" he ranted, ignoring her question. "Interfering in other people's lives."

"Don't assign your relationship problems to me, pal. The blame lies with you."

"Blah, blah, blah. You pretend you're this big sexual expert. Go find your inner goddess and all that crap. Well, you know what I think?"

"What do you think, Dave? If you can indeed think," Callie challenged, clenching her jaw against the anger knifing her gut.

"I did some research on you. I found out you don't even have a boyfriend. Why's that?"

"None of your business."

"I think that deep down inside you're afraid of intimacy. I think you like to talk about sex and give glib advice because you wouldn't know what to do with a real man if you got your dirty hands on one."

Was she afraid of intimacy?

The caller's accusations struck a chord. While she'd had her fair share of lovers, she'd never been in love. All her relationships had been light and fun just the way she liked them. None of her love affairs had lasted more than six months.

In fact, she wasn't even sure that she believed in romantic love. Her parents' marriage had been a total disaster. She always thought that Hollywood love-at-first-sight stuff was just pie-in-the-sky daydreaming. Sex was real, yeah baby. But romantic love? Just make-believe malarkey.

Shake it off, Callie. Don't let this jerk throw you off. That's what he wants.

"And I suppose you consider yourself a real man." She was taunting him and she knew it, but she wasn't going to allow her insecurities to undermine her self-confidence.

Her caller guffawed. "You have no idea the things I could do to you."

His ominous tone raised the hairs on the nape of her neck. "Are you threatening me?"

"All I'm saying is that you are going to be out on your book tour for three weeks. Away from the protection of your precious crew. You'd better watch yourself."

"Are you the person who's been sending menacing letters to the station?" she demanded.

Dave did not answer.

Callie took a deep breath, preparing to launch into a tirade and tell the idiot what a dirty-dog coward he really was. She intended on daring him to come down to the station and meet her in person, when Barb pulled the plug on the call and cut to commercial.

"What did you do that for?" Callie asked, ripping off her headphones and turning her pent-up frustrations onto the engineer. "I was about to give that a-hole the dressing down he deserved."

Barb gesticulated toward the glass partition.

Glaring fiercely, Callie snapped her head around to see what Barb was pointing at and found herself eye to eye with a man so magnetic the breath left her body in one long whoosh of air.

Their gazes clashed like steel swords.

En garde, *big boy.*

Callie's focus narrowed onto his face and a shiver of expectation rolled over her.

Oh my. She brought two fingers up to trace her blazing hot lips. He was magnificent.

Imposingly tall and as muscular as a warrior. His midnight-black hair, clipped close to his skull in a precision military cut, gave him a steadfast appearance reinforced by the chiseled lines of his jaw.

His cheekbones were high and sculpted, his features decidedly Nordic but his eyes weren't Scandinavian blue. No, they were black as pitch and eerily intelligent.

And his mouth, ah, his poetic, artistic mouth, gave him away.

That full, soft pliant mouth told her everything she needed to know about his soul. While he was strong and brave on the outside, his sensuous mouth whispered that he was kindhearted and caring on the inside.

She had absolutely no trouble imagining him lying

naked in her bed. She could actually see his big masculine hands on her bare thighs, feel his rough calluses
skimming along her tender flesh.

And he would have calluses.

She could feel him brush his thumb against her
inner leg, his fingers inching closer to her moist hot
center, not quite touching her there. She saw him dipping his dark head down to where his feverish breath
heated her skin. Goose bumps dotted her legs and she
rose up, thrusting her pelvis toward him, moaning for
more, urging him to go on, but then he sternly shook
his head.

No. No. No.

And Callie found herself jolted out of her imaginary
bedroom. She dropped back down into her body at the
radio station, feeling woozy and disoriented.

She shook her head. What had just happened?

He was watching her closely, almost as if reading her
mind and he frowned in disapproval.

*Sorry dude, can't help the direction of my errant
fantasies.*

He drew himself up even taller. He had to be several
inches over six-foot. He seemed a throwback to another
time, a different era. Where honor and chivalry were
paramount. Where stalwart knights defended the virtue
of fair maidens. Where loyalty was rewarded and gal-
lantry was second nature.

Callie's heart raced. She could literally feel his energy, surging outward through the glass partition, drawing her to him.

She'd never experienced such instant chemistry with

anyone and the feeling was exciting and thrilling and quite terrifying all at the same time.

The moment was so surreal Callie had to blink twice to make sure he hadn't sprung to life, fully realized from her gray matter.

Who was he? Where had he come from? What was he doing here?

And that's when she realized he was holding up a piece of paper scribbled with the words: Get her off the air now!

Oh no.

Crap. This was the bodyguard Molly Anne had spoken of. Waltzing in, taking over, already putting himself in charge of her life.

And from the uncompromising expression on his rugged face Callie could tell that this was how he thought it was going to be.

3

LUKE WISHED that he had the power to reach into the switchboard, snatch the cowardly caller by the throat, yank him through the phone lines and confront him face-to-face. He'd never been able to stomach men who bullied women.

What he yearned to do now was plant Callie securely behind his back, then double up his fists and challenge any and everyone who intended her harm. But before he had time to ponder the unexpectedness of his emotional response, Callie thundered from the soundproof booth, shoulders squared, eyes flaming, saucy tongue in high gear.

"Just who in the hell do you think you are?" she demanded, skidding to a halt less than a foot away and sinking her hands on her hips.

She was one fiery beauty with her bohemian hair and her silver hoop earrings sprouting brash turquoise feathers that stroked her jaw line. She was quite mesmerizing in a very unconventional way. She had almond-shaped eyes that made Luke think of dangerous secrets and long-hidden desires.

This woman was a force of nature and the power of

her personality reeled him in. He cocked an eyebrow and coolly gave her the once-over.

She possessed the spirited cheek of a charming out-law and she rattled him to the bone. But he wasn't about to let her know that. He prayed that his controlled facial expression managed to belie the inferno she stoked inside his belly. Because if this potent, sexy woman had any inkling of the irreverent thoughts spinning in his head, he was done for.

Her eyes widened as she stared at him. Suddenly it dawned on Luke they were dressed almost identically.

Black top. Green camouflage bottoms. Combat boots.

Never mind that his pants were loose fitting and that her miniskirt was so tight it could have doubled as a dew rag. Essentially, they were wearing the same outfit. It was a very odd sensation, seeing a feminized version of himself standing right before his eyes. Except his clothes were real solider fatigues whereas her scant costume was nothing more than a fashion statement.

"Wow," Zack said, from behind Luke. "Look at you two. Twinzees."

She was a teensy little thing. Five-two at the most and she couldn't have weighed more than a hundred pounds. Her entire body would have fit into one leg of his pants and here she was challenging him as if she were three times his size. Courageous, bold. He admired those qualities, admired them a lot. He also admired the way her smile was just a little bit crooked, as if she knew a secret joke and wasn't about to let the rest of the world in on it.

Definitely a red flag moment.

This was not good. He could not be attracted to the woman he'd been hired to protect. And why did she have to smell so good? Like cinnamon and ginger and something fuller, richer, more feminine. He had an urge to lick her skin and see if she tasted as good as she smelled.

Ah hell. He was getting a boner.

Luke gritted his teeth, struggling to restrain his arousal. *Face it, Cardasian. You are so damned desperate for sex that anyone of the feminine persuasion can get you hard.*

But he knew that simply wasn't true. He had walked past a hundred gorgeous women out on the streets of New York without getting the same response. Nope, for some perverse twist of nature, it was this pint-size dynamo who inflamed him.

"No one pulls the plug on my show without my permission," she barked like a drill sergeant.

"I believe I just did." He glowered, getting into his anger. Anger was an appropriate alternative to lust. He put his hands on his hips, mirroring her aggressive body language, giving her a dose of her pique. Her spunkiness made him smile. How could he stay a hard-ass when she looked so darn cute? He reached over and pantomimed flicking a chip off her shoulder.

"Hey!"

"Play nice, Callie. This is your new bodyguard," the tall cool blonde said.

"You have got to be kidding." Callie snorted and shook her head.

The blonde extended her hand to Luke. "I'm Molly Anne Armstrong by the way. The Midnight Ryder's business manager."

"Luke Cardasian."

The woman's hand was limp, but she smiled sweetly and Luke overlooked her dead-fish handshake.

"I don't like him," Callie drawled in her smooth whiskey accent. The sound of her lodged inside his gut and seeped slowly throughout his system like maple syrup drizzled over hotcakes.

He shifted his gaze from Molly Anne to Callie. He appreciated her bluntness. You knew where you stood with this one. No pussyfooting around sensitive issues. Something told Luke she would shake hands like a champion prizefighter. Hard, firm, determined to win at all costs. Except she wasn't about to shake hands with him. She looked as if she would rather French-kiss a rattlesnake.

"Don't hold back on my account," he said. "Tell me how you really feel."

She was spunky. He liked her even if she didn't like him.

"Chill out for a minute, Callie," Molly Anne said. "You're just irritated because Luke had Barb cut off that threatening caller."

"Yes I am. And what's wrong with that?" Callie asked. "It's my show. He has no business stepping in and acting so high-handed."

"I beg to differ. He is exactly what you need. Who wants a pushover bodyguard?" pressed Molly Anne.

"I don't want a bodyguard at all." Callie hardened her look.

"I had your engineer cut off the caller for your own safety," Luke explained. "Not to mention the best interests of the radio station. You were provoking the guy and you have no clue what he's capable of."

"I was not provoking him. I was handling him just fine. I didn't need your intervention."

Luke shrugged. "Too bad. You got it."

Oh, that pissed her off. Her eyes narrowed and she wagged a finger in his face. "I am not having some two-bit soldier boy telling me how to run my show."

Two-bit soldier boy? Now she was just trying to get even.

"That's a low blow," he said.

"Can't take the heat? Get out of my kitchen." She doubled her fists at her sides and he wondered why she was so inclined to fight. What had happened to turn her so pugilistic? Not that he minded. Luke enjoyed a worthy opponent.

"Well, guess what?" he said. "I won't have some demanding prima donna telling me how best to do my job."

"Prima donna? Are you calling me a prima donna?"

"If the moniker fits…"

"You don't act like a bodyguard to me. You're too contentious. What precisely are your qualifications?" she asked. "Exactly how long have you been a bodyguard?"

"In truth? You're my first client."

"What?" She scowled at Molly Anne. "You hired a virgin bodyguard? Oh, lovely. That's rich."

"I was a Navy M.P.," Luke interjected. "And for the last six years I've been guiding aid workers and the news media through one of the most volatile countries on the planet. I think that qualifies me for baby-sitting a smart-mouthed shock jock."

"Baby-sitting?" She glared, hissing the word through clenched teeth. Apparently she liked this word even less than prima donna.

"Baby-sitting," he echoed, staring her down.

"A deranged caller is threatening my life and you think that all you'll be doing is sitting around on your duff?"

"Yep."

"Get rid of him!" Callie said to Molly Anne.

"Take it easy, sweetheart." He had to confess he was just messing with her now. Intentionally riling her just to see those almond eyes narrow and that crooked little mouth dive down in anger.

"I am *not* your sweetheart," she raged, "I'm no one's sweetheart. Got it? And don't tell me to take it easy."

"Why are you so scared of me?" he asked, slowing his speech, trying to read the woman behind the outrage.

"I'm not scared of you!" She looked taken aback by his suggestion. He knew he had hit her insecurities dead-on.

"Then why are you picking a fight?"

"News flash, scared people run away from altercations," she said. "They don't pick fights."

"Oh yes they do. Some people pick fights hoping the other fella will run away first."

"He's impossible," Callie exclaimed and threw her arms in the air. "I simply will not work with him."

Molly Anne addressed Zack. "I like your brother. He holds his ground. Callie steamrollers right over most people."

"Oh, Luke will never let her get away with that stuff," Zack said. "He loves squaring off against people. He's a real crusader. Always looking for someone to reform."

"He'll have his work cut out for him." Molly Anne chuckled.

"Hello!" Callie huffed, waved her arms. "We're standing right here."

Yes she was. Not two feet from Luke.

And looking mighty sexy in her indignation. He took a second gander at her compact little body. Her biceps and triceps were firm and shapely, a testament to her commitment to regular strength training. He approved. Her bare abdomen was flat and taut. Her navel sported a silver belly ring. Which he did not approve of. But in spite of being a lean machine, she still had curves. Generous hips, a high derriere, nice breasts.

Spend time with me, her sumptuous figure beckoned. He could not, would not, but that didn't mean he didn't dream. In a blinding flash, he saw her in his mind's eye, standing naked underneath a waterfall, her strangely colored purple-pink hair plastered against the nape of her neck, the swell of her nipples glistening wetly.

Mentally, Luke tracked her imaginary, but highly sensuous movements, as she cocked her head and took the full brunt of the splashing cascade upon her chest. He slid his gaze down the curvy lines of her slender shoulders and watched the water bead over her rich skin.

His imagination exploded. He envisioned himself shucking off his own clothing and joining her under that waterfall. He fantasized that he was snaking out a hand, grabbing her lithe wrist and hauling her hard against his bare slick body, holding her a willing captive in his embrace.

Her body heat was in sharp contrast to the cool water.

He sank his teeth into her bottom lip and sucked it roughly into his mouth. He wanted more. Yes, yes. Inside his addled brain, he took her mouth in his in one long, soul-searching kiss. She felt so warm and human in his embrace. He had been too long without a woman. He'd forgotten how amazingly soft they were. Her skin was so delicate, her fingers adorably small. The illusion was so vivid, so real, Luke began to worry that his flight of fancy had morphed into a full-blown hallucination.

"Snap out of it," he growled and violently shook his head. It was only when everyone turned to stare that Luke realized he had spoken aloud.

"What?" Callie bristled, obviously thinking he'd been talking to her. "What did you say to me?"

"Nothing," Luke mumbled, hating that his reverie had cost him the upper hand. "Nothing at all."

"You're blushing." Callie gave him the once-over as if she was a motorcycle cop and he was a New Year's Eve reveler who'd had one Sex-on-the-Beach too many.

"No, I'm not," Luke denied even as his ears caught fire.

"Then why is your face red? Do you have high blood pressure? The last thing I need is a virgin bodyguard who's about to stroke out."

He wished she would stop saying the word "virgin." Especially with regards to him. "I don't have high blood pressure, dammit. Or at least I didn't until I met you."

"There's the door." She pointed. "You don't like the situation. Hit it."

The woman could get on a guy's last nerve. Obviously he could not accept this job. Not when the attraction was testing every ounce of self-discipline he possessed. Not when he wanted to wring her lovely little neck at the very same moment he simultaneously wanted to kiss her silly.

He had to refuse the assignment. For his own peace of mind. Plus, he had a legitimate excuse for weaseling out so no one would guess the real reason he couldn't hang. He would tell her if he wasn't allowed full control over the security details for the entire book tour then he was well within his rights to cancel the contract.

"You're absolutely correct," he said. "This arrangement isn't going to work."

"Wait a minute." Callie's nostrils flared. "Are you firing *me?*"

"That's right."

"You can't fire me. I fired you first."

"This isn't a case of one-upsmanship."

"Fine, then I fire you."

He looked at Molly Anne. "I'm sorry Ms. Armstrong, for wasting your time, but Cardasian Security cannot insure Ms. Ryder's safety if she insists on questioning my authority and if I can't insure her safety, we cannot in good conscience accept this contract."

"There's no time to make new travel arrangements with a new bodyguard. Our flight leaves in eight hours and the ticket has already been issued in your name," Molly Anne argued.

"I'm sorry for your inconvenience," he said.

"But we have already paid your firm fifty percent of your fee."

This was news to him but Luke hadn't been home

long enough to sit down with Zack and go over the accounts. He was at a distinct disadvantage in the negotiations. He glanced at his brother. "Give Ms. Armstrong her money back."

Zack looked sheepish. "Can I talk to you for a sec? In private."

Luke didn't like the sound of this. "Please excuse us a moment, ladies."

"If you keep on walking it will be hunky-dory with me," Callie hollered after him.

Don't lose your temper. If you lose your temper she wins. He stepped out into the hall. Zack followed.

"Why can't you give them their money back?" Luke demanded once the door had closed behind them.

"Um." Zack stuck his hands in his pockets and jingled his change. "I sort of spent it on the down payment for the Hummer."

"And we don't even have fifteen grand left in the bank?"

"Not really." Zack winced and cringed. "I also paid the yearly fire insurance on the office building and barely met payroll."

Somehow Luke had known what his brother was going to say. He shook his head. No wonder their parents had called, begging him to come home and help Zack with the business. Left to his own devices his brother would bankrupt Cardasian Personal Security Services within the year.

"So what you're telling me is that in order to make ends meet we really have no choice. I have to take this assignment."

"Yeah, kinda."

Luke growled. "Or you could go on the road with her and I could stay here and go through the books. Try and squeeze out every spare nickel."

"But I'm in the middle of planning a wedding, re-member."

"Belinda's planning a wedding."

"I promised her I'd go with her to pick out the cake. Plus, her parents are coming into town next week and they're taking us to dinner."

"What about Carl or Jim?"

"They're already both on lengthy assignments."

"I don't believe this." Luke ran a palm down his face. "Once again you've left me dangling with my butt in the breeze."

"Hey," Zack said defensively. "Don't get on your high horse. I was the one who was here when Dad had his heart attack. You were the one who was off gallivant-ing around Africa."

"Excuse me, but I was helping to guide innocent people trying to do good in a country torn by war."

"Or maybe you were just hiding out."

"What's that supposed to mean?"

Zack shrugged. "It wasn't your war to get involved with. Why were you even there?"

"You know why. I couldn't say no to Mukasi. We spent half our life in that country. Are you telling me you don't care what happens to those people?"

"No," Zack said. "You know I do care. I just don't want you judging me. I was here, you weren't. I spent the money how I saw fit."

"Yes and now because of it I have to guard that hellion in there." Luke pointed toward the door. "On the road 24/7 for three miserable weeks."

"I don't see what you're getting so bent out of shape about. You gotta admit Callie Ryder is twice as hot in person as she is on that billboard."

Her supercharged hotness was exactly the reason Luke did not want to accept the job, but he wasn't about to tell Zack that. He was certain he could control himself around temptation.

Unlike some people. He glared at his brother.

"Besides," Zack said. "I think you've finally met your match. Both of you are decisive and direct and determined to be in charge."

"Are you kidding? We're like fire and ice. I felt the tension the minute we laid eyes on each other."

"Sexual tension is a good thing, bro. That means there's passion brewing."

"It's not sexual tension," Luke denied. "She just gets under my skin."

"Same thing."

"Knock it off."

"Can't you see it's kismet?" Zack teased, clasping his palms together under his chin and batting his eyelashes in a silly romantic gesture.

"Shut up." He could hear the sound of his own teeth grinding.

"I mean, hell, what other woman on earth would be dressed exactly like you? Face it. She's the one. She's your soul mate."

Luke started to pole-vault down his brother's throat for that ridiculous crack until he saw Zack grinning, obviously trying to get his goat. He forced a smile in return. "Fine…great…okay. I'll guard Ms. Diva. Just don't expect me to like it."

SHE HAD TO MAKE HIM LEAVE.

There was no way she was going to put up with Luke Cardasian's strong-arm tactics for three interminable weeks. It wasn't just because he was one of the most irritating men she had ever met. Which he was. No, her need to get him out of her life ran much deeper.

He scared her.

Not because he was so big and imposing. Not because he possessed the mental toughness of a bulldog. Not even because his self-control barely masked a powder keg of emotions. What really frightened her was the weird sensation that rippled at the back of her knees whenever he looked deeply into her eyes. Because nothing terrified Callie more than the idea of laying herself vulnerable in front of some man.

And a stranger at that.

It was the main reason she preferred physical closeness to emotional intimacy. Sex she could handle. It was the cuddling and snuggling and confidence sharing that did her in. When you got intimate with someone, that's when you got hurt. If you kept your emotional armor in place, kept the pillow talk light and never revealed anything important about yourself, then there wasn't much a lover could use to stab you in the back.

But what if you found someone you could really let down your guard with? Wouldn't that be wonderful?

No. No it wouldn't. While she might secretly long to

backtrack and rediscover the girl she'd once been before she'd become the Midnight Ryder, Callie resisted
lifting up the corner of that particular rug to examine
what she'd been sweeping underneath it all these years.

She had to get rid of Cardasian and that's all there
was to it. Before he became her undoing. Unfortunately,
when Callie had called Roger McKee to lodge her com-
plaint about Cardasian, she received little sympathy
from the station manager. Roger had merely reiterated
what Molly Anne had already told her. She could either
accept the bodyguard or pay for the book tour out of her
own pocket.

Or—she'd mentally added to Roger's limited list of
options as she hung up—she could piss off the big
burly bodyguard so he would quit. It shouldn't take
much to make Cardasian mad enough to storm off in a
huff. She could tell he disliked her almost as much as
she disliked him.

But how best to execute her plan?

*Play to your talents. Be outrageous. Shock the pants
off him.*

Good idea. She'd already figured out he shocked
rather easily. For the duration of their cross-country
flight to Los Angeles he'd sat rigidly beside her in the
first class cabin. Stony as old Teddy Roosevelt on Mount
Rushmore.

Big, imposing, silent. He'd barely spoken ten words.

Luckily, Molly Anne was seated behind and across
the aisle from them, plus she was asleep, so no interfer-
ence from that source. It was the perfect time to put her
get-rid-of-Cardasian plot into play.

"Tell me something," Callie murmured in the most seductive voice she could muster as the plane circled over LAX.

He inclined his head, waiting for her to continue. She flipped her copy of *Cosmo* closed and leaned forward to drop the magazine into her travel bag. Just to unnerve Luke, she made sure the top of her head grazed his forearm during the maneuver. What she didn't count on, though, was the sharp zing of awareness.

"You got a girlfriend or what, Cardasian?"

He did not answer.

She straightened, purposefully not readjusting the hem of the miniskirt that had ridden up high on her thigh. She smiled engagingly. Still, he said nothing.

"What? You givin' me the silent treatment?"

He shook his head.

"No, you're not giving me the silent treatment or no, you don't have a girlfriend?"

He telegraphed her a look. *Shut up and mind your own business*.

But Callie did neither. "No girlfriend. Got it. Boyfriend then?"

He frowned and vigorously shook his head.

"Ah, so you're not gay. I guess that means that either you're into one-night stands or you're celibate."

Nothing. She could have wrung more conversation from a boulder.

"I'm guessing celibate. You strike me as too much of a Goody Two-shoes for one-night stands."

From the back pocket of the seat in front of them, he plucked up the copy of *USA Today* that he had already perused three times and snapped it open with an angry flick of his wrist.

"Is it just my imagination," she asked, lowering her voice and angling her upper body toward him. "Or are the tips of your ears turning bright red? Am I embarrassing you?"

He grunted but did not glance at her. His teeth were clamped so tightly that his jaw muscles bunched. He was hanging on to his temper with spider-web control.

"Honestly, Luke, no need to blush. You shouldn't be ashamed of your celibacy. Happens to the best of us from time to time." He was blushing and he hadn't denied it. How sweet. He really must be celibate. What delightful ammunition. "Just between you and me how long *has* it been since you got laid?"

"I won't discuss my sex life."

"Or lack thereof?"

He stared at her, murder in his eyes. Ooh goodie, she was getting to him. But damn if he wasn't getting to her, as well.

His dark, moody, high-voltage scowl caused her heart to shoot up into her throat and then immediately plummet back down into her stomach. A runaway elevator. His hard-edged gaze nailed her to the seat and she felt as if the wind had been slapped from her lungs.

Maybe she ought to back off a bit. At least until they were safely on the ground and her hands had stopped quaking.

By the time they were in the terminal the tension between them was thick as July in New Orleans. Muggy, moody, portentous.

Even Molly Anne noticed. "What's up between you and the bodyguard?" she asked when they detoured to the airport terminal ladies' room after the plane had landed. She took off her fake glasses and polished the lenses with a paper towel.

Callie stood in front of the mirror, spiking her hair with her fingers, making sure she looked as punkish as possible. She slid her favorite cologne—*Sinful*—from her purse and dabbed a bit behind each ear. One way or the other, she was going to give Luke a run for his money.

"I think I rub him the wrong way," she said.

"Well start rubbing him the right way, will you? We need him."

Callie rolled her eyes. She needed Cardasian like… well…like a trout needed a Harley.

For the first time, her mother's favorite saying made total sense. She could defend herself. She had no use for a bodyguard and the sooner she goaded him into quitting, the better. Learning about his celibacy had given her an advantage and she knew exactly how to ratchet up the heat.

"Take it easy on Luke. If all goes well on this tour, you could very possibly be getting Buck Bryson's time slot."

Callie stopped preening, pursed her mouth and stared at Molly Anne's reflection. "What?"

Molly Anne nodded. "Roger's backing you all the way. With him in your corner and the soaring ratings of *Let's Talk About Sex*, if the sales of your book are good, too, the board of directors is bound to want to retool your show for the morning slot."

"Really?" Callie squeaked.

They clasped each other by the shoulders and danced an excited little jig right there in the bathroom.

"This is what we've been working so hard for all these years. With the a.m. slot you can do more education, less titillation like you've always wanted," Molly Anne said. "So I'm begging you, please don't do anything that could screw this up."

All the more reason to ditch Luke. With the way he agitated her, sooner or later she was bound to take a misstep. The quicker she got rid of him, the better. For the sake of her mental health, as much as for her career.

Luke had been waiting for them to come out of the ladies' room, his arms crossed over his chest. Silently, he fell in step behind them, his watchful gaze scanning the disembarking crowd for potential threats.

Too bad he had to go. The guy was one hell of a hottie.

"I'll meet you guys at baggage claim," Molly Anne said and flipped open her cell phone. "I have a few calls to make. Publicity arrangements to verify, that sort of thing."

Molly Anne took off down the concourse, which surprised Callie a little but she wasn't really thinking about her friend. Her mind was on getting rid of Luke. Callie tossed her head and made a beeline for the small sundries store. Luke stuck to her elbow like he was Velcro.

"Where are you going?" he asked.

"I need something." She stopped in front of the medicinal and personal hygiene section. Hmm, where was it? Arms akimbo, she searched the shelves. Sunscreen and lip balm and those tiny pink motion-sickness pills. Travel toothbrushes and pocket-size tissues and miniature bottles of aspirin stickered with exorbitant price tags.

And then she spotted what she was searching for, tucked discreetly into a back corner. She didn't reach for them. Instead, she pretended to peruse the shelf until Luke unwittingly rose to the bait.

"What are you looking for?" he asked at last.

"It's personal. In fact, why don't you go wait by the magazine stand?" She made shooing motions at him. "Check out the latest issue of *Hotbed Honeys* or something."

"I don't read those kinds of publications." He bristled.

"Sure you do. You're celibate, aren't you. If you're not having sex you've got to be jacking off."

"Ms. Ryder," he said gruffly. "I'd appreciate it if you'd keep your voice down."

"Hit a sore spot, did I? How many times a day do you masturbate?"

"What!" He looked mortified.

"Come on, confess."

He glared. "Hush."

She cocked her head and gave him her naughtiest smile. Darn if a little blue vein wasn't popping out on his forehead.

"You're enjoying this, aren't you?"

"Sure am." She winked.

"I can assure you that you're not going to chase me off with your frank talk. I've been hired to stay by your side."

"Suit yourself." She shrugged and turned her attention back to the display racks. They were standing shoulder to shoulder, staring at the wall of hygiene products. Her heart was thudding. She didn't know about him, but all this talk of masturbation was certainly getting to her. Luke was so close she could feel the body heat rolling off his large frame in waves.

Why did the thought of teasing him excite her so much? All she wanted was to be such a pain in his keester that he would quit the job and go back to New York.

"Is this what you're looking for?" He held up a box of tampons.

"No."

He swiftly returned the box to the shelf. "You said it was personal."

"It is."

"There's feminine itch cream on the shelf next to the deodorant." He pointed. "And freshness spray, whatever that is."

"Don't need those, either."

"So what do you need?" he asked.

Did he have any idea how loaded that question was? Callie slanted him a sideways glance to see how much innuendo was in his face. His innocent expression almost had her rethinking her fiendish plan to sexually embarrass him in public. Almost.

"Condoms," she said in a loud voice so anyone standing in the vicinity would overhear them. "I need a box of condoms."

"What for?" he asked.

"What do you mean what for? Condoms have only one use."

"I mean," he said, lowering his voice to an urgent

whisper, the tips of his ears tinged red again. She was really starting to like that telltale blush. It was quaint and sort of gallant. "You need a partner to use those with."

"Why, Luke, are you offering to break your celibacy and become my road trip release valve?"

"No!"

"But you just said…" she trailed off.

"You're twisting my words and you know it."

She smiled slyly and moistened her lips. His gaze fixed on her tongue, watching its every flick. Oh-ho! Mr. I-Keep-My-Emotions-Under-Tight-Control was attracted to her. A powerful piece of information indeed.

"What I meant to say," he said, tensing his jaw muscles in that way of his, looking mighty unhappy with the topic of conversation. "If you plan on taking a lover while you're on this book tour, I insist you allow me to have his background thoroughly checked out first."

"Wouldn't it be much easier," she said, drawing on her bold sexpert persona to push him over the edge, "if you would just volunteer to be my lover?"

She skimmed her fingernails lightly over his forearm. And it was not her imagination. The big man actually shuddered. There was sexual tension between them, no question. But she really didn't intend on seducing him. She just wanted to chase him away. But now, she couldn't stop thinking about making love to this juicy hunk of man. She kept wondering if he really was as chaste and pure of heart as he seemed.

"What size should I get?" She stroked the box of condoms. "Large? Extra large? Please don't tell me we'll be needing a small."

"I know what you're doing," he growled. "And it's not going to work."

"Do you?" Her tone was pure whiskey and honey, low and suggestive.

"You're trying to rattle me, put me off my game, cause me to make a mistake."

"Now why would I do that?" Callie asked, reaching up to finger his tie.

He'd worn a dark business suit on the plane but Callie preferred him in his camouflage pants and combat boots and tight black T-shirt. What she thought of as his rough-and-tough look.

"Because," he said, "having a bodyguard puts you in a submissive position and you can't stand the thought of that. You have to be in charge and you're trying to wrest back control any way you can."

Oh, Mr. Smarty Pants Bodyguard. Well fine. If he refused to let her sexual innuendo run him off, she'd just have to find another way to get rid of him.

Callie plucked the condoms off the shelf and took a ten-dollar bill from her wallet, then handed Luke both the money and the prophylactics.

He stared at her.

"Buy these for me, will you?"

Without waiting for his response, she sashayed over to the newsstand, picked up a copy of *Vogue* and pretended to be totally engrossed.

She sneaked a quick glance into the shoplifting mirror perched on the wall above her head to see what he would do. Luke stood there a minute, finally muttered something under his breath and got in line for the checkout. There were two people in the queue ahead of him. She had to wait until the right moment to make her move. He watched her closely until he stepped up to the register and the clerk engaged him in conversation. Looking flustered, he laid the condoms on the counter.

The second Callie saw his concentration shift from her to the clerk, she jammed the magazine back on the shelf and darted into the terminal. The crowd flowing past swallowed her up.

Ha! Pulse galloping, she turned at the next corner, pushed through the revolving doors and found herself deposited outside on the street near the taxi stand. *Brilliant Callie, now what?*

4

LUKE HAD BEEN in precarious situations before and he'd always managed to survive. This time, he assured himself was no different. But it was. He could handle the treacherous danger in Limbasa far easier than he could handle the audacious Callie Ryder and her alluring feminine scent. He was way out of his league.

She knew exactly what she was doing. Smelling too good, talking sexy, trying her damnedest to get a rise out of him.

And risen he had. She was nearly driving him out of his mind whispering about condoms and celibacy and dirty magazines. He winced just thinking about how swiftly he got a hard-on whenever he was near her.

The sassy woman's enticing aroma of nutmeg and ginger and cinnamon made him ache to brush up against her. She smelled like a dream. Like home. And for a man who often felt out of step with the rest of the world, home was a deadly inviting scent.

Luke shifted in line at the checkout counter and glanced over at Callie. She was deeply engrossed in her magazine and he found his gaze tracing down the length of her back. She wore a formfitting stretch knit black blouse and a mouthwatering short crimson skirt that set his blood boiling. And even though she was petite in stature, she was still three-fourths long lean legs.

Her skin was firm and bronzed, her stomach flat, waist narrow and her breasts were the perfect size of ripe peaches. She moved as if she owned the world. Lithe, supple, confident in her abilities to please. He blew out his breath. Man, she was something to look at. When he realized two-thirds of the men in the store were also staring at her, he had the compelling urge to double up his fists and blacken their ogling eyes.

Highly unprofessional. This protective surge he felt toward her went far beyond duty and bordered on stupid. She shifted and glanced at him over her shoulder, winked and then went back to her magazine.

Lust tortured him. His body hardened and he had to close his eyes and steel his jaw in order to fight off the boner.

"May I help you, sir," asked the polite caramel-skinned gentleman behind the register. Nervously, Luke fumbled with the condoms and dropped them onto the counter.

"Is this the kind that you want?" the clerk asked in heavily accented English. "Ribbed for her pleasure?"

Luke nodded and he felt his cheeks scorch. How had he let himself get rooked into buying condoms for her? And was she really thinking about hooking up with a stranger for a road fling. He winced. He hoped not. It could present a security nightmare. The clerk quickly sacked the condoms in a brown paper bag, made change and gave him his purchase.

"Come again, sir," the clerk said and then laughed at his own joke.

Luke stalked away from the counter, stomping over to the magazine stand, determined to set Callie straight about his function. He was her bodyguard, not her personal shopper, not her roadie, not the man she was going to use to scratch her sexual itch.

Hey, wait a minute. Where was she? Puzzled, Luke searched the corners of the open store. She was small, but not that small. A panicky sensation clutched his gut.

She'd already been to the ladies' room with Molly Anne when they'd gotten off the plane so he doubted she'd gone back in there. Could someone have snatched her? If they had, he certainly felt sorry for the kidnappers.

But it wasn't funny. He'd committed the bodyguard's cardinal sin. He'd lost sight of his protectee.

TWO MINUTES LATER, Callie's impulsive flight from the terminal was starting to look pretty stupid. She hadn't thought this thing through. She had simply been irritated with Luke's high-handedness and wanted to prove she could outwit him. And just maybe shame the prideful man into quitting.

Right. Now where to from here? She probably ought to go find Molly Anne and help her redeem their luggage.

A Los Angeles city bus lumbered past. Callie blinked, unable to believe what she was seeing. Her picture plastered on the side of the bus.

Callie Ryder Gives Shockingly Good Sex.

For one moment, she felt exactly like the Carrie Bradshaw character from the opening sequence of *Sex and the City,* overwhelmed by her newfound popularity.

The poster on the side of the bus was a smaller version of the one in Times Square. Callie knew Molly Anne had done advance publicity for the tour, but she was openmouthed to learn her business manager's efforts had included advertising on public transportation. Molly Anne was a dynamo at PR. She was definitely going to have to give the woman a raise.

It was oddly surreal. Seeing her star on the rise on the opposite side of the country. This was no fluke. She had officially arrived. But she had no time to fully absorb the moment or appreciate the significance of it or even feel sad that she had no one to share it with.

"Omigosh, it's her!" a woman squealed.

"Her who?" asked another woman. "Is it a movie star?"

Callie glanced around, trying to see which celebrity the women had spotted.

"No, look, look," said the first woman. "Her picture was on the side of the bus that just went by. It's that radio deejay from *Let's Talk About Sex*. She's standing right over there."

They were talking about her? Callie peeked over at the women. They appeared to be in their late teens or early twenties, Callie's targeted demographic.

"Callie Ryder!" exclaimed the women in unison and rushed her.

The next thing she knew, she was surrounded not just by the two women but also by their entire group, a cheerful gaggle of sorority sisters from Tulane on their way to tour Hollywood.

"We just love your show," said one woman admiringly.

"Can you give me some advice about my boyfriend?" asked a third.

"What method of birth control do you think works best?"

"What does it really mean when a guy sleeps with you on the first date and then never calls?"

They crowded in on her. Callie felt besieged. In New York she occasionally ran across an avid fan, but she'd never experienced anything like this on the streets of Manhattan. A claustrophobic sensation squeezed her chest and she wanted to scream at them to back off so she could breathe.

This is what you always wanted, remember? To spread the word to young women everywhere. Sex is fun. Dive right in and make no excuses for enjoying yourself.

Well, apparently they were getting the message loud and clear. Problem was, Callie hadn't expected this kind of reaction. She gulped and took a step back. The young women went with her. She tried to take another step back and trod on someone's toe.

"Oh, oh, I'm so sorry." Callie put out a hand to cup the woman's elbow.

"Please don't apologize." The young woman giggled. "Now I can tell everyone the Midnight Ryder scuffed my Jimmy Choos."

"Please, step on my foot, too," someone else begged.

Okay, this was officially frightening. Callie was starting to regret running away from Luke. *Come on, you're the Midnight Ryder. Shake it off. Suck it up. You're tough and bold and brave and nothing gets to you.*

"Um...I...have to..." she said, but the twenty or thirty coeds grouped around her never let her get a word in edgewise. Just when Callie thought she was going to have to throw back her head and scream in order to get their attention, a deep masculine voice broke through the chick chatter.

"Excuse me, ladies," Luke said.

Immediately, the tittering women parted. He held out an arm to Callie and gratefully, she grasped it.

"You ready to go, sweetheart?" he asked rather possessively as if he were her boyfriend.

What was that all about? And why did she get this soft swoony sensation deep in the pit of her stomach at the thought of having him as her boyfriend? She didn't even do boyfriends.

Her heart was knocking and her breathing was shallow. She didn't know if her unexpected emotions sprang from what had just happened with her fans or from Luke's knight-in-shining-armor act or a little bit of both.

"Thank you for rescuing me," she said, once they were back in the terminal, out of earshot of the young women.

Luke interrupted her before she went any further. "Save it."

She was startled by the fury in his eyes. "What's wrong?"

"You have to ask?"

"You're mad because I ditched you?"

His scowl said it all. "I only helped you out because you are under my protection and I have a duty to you. But no more. It ends here. I can't work for a woman who does not accept my authority. You have nothing but blatant disregard for me and what I do."

She hadn't expected him to get so angry. Nor had she expected to be so turned on by his anger. His face looked volcanic, as if ready to spew molten lava, and all she could think about was how much she wished he would just kiss her. She opened her mouth to argue, to defend her actions, but Luke held up his palm for silence.

"Because of your irresponsible behavior, I can't trust you. Nor can I assure your safety. I won't put my reputation at risk. I will return your fee. You'll have to find someone else to supply your security needs. Because as of this moment, I quit."

"Luke…I…I…" she stammered.

But he'd already turned and stalked away, headed for the ticket counter. He was going home? Right now? But this was a good thing. It was what she wanted. Wasn't it? Why then did she feel like such an ass?

Luke stopped abruptly, turned around and marched toward her. He was coming back!

"Yes?" she whispered when he stood directly in front of her.

"Here's your damned condoms. Enjoy them in good health."

She clasped the brown paper bag he'd thrust into her hands and stared after Luke's retreating back, too surprised to know how she felt.

"Callie!"

Molly Anne's voice had her swinging around to find her business manager coming toward her with what appeared to be a television reporter and a camera crew following a few paces behind.

What the hell?

"Where did you go?" Molly Anne asked. "We've been waiting for you in baggage claim for over twenty minutes."

"We?"

Molly Anne stepped close and murmured under her breath so the reporter couldn't hear. "I had an interview set up for you to promote the book tour."

"It would have been nice if you had clued me in," Callie said.

"They wanted to catch you on the move. As a surprise."

"Ambush is more like it."

"You're going to be a superstar. It's time you started acting like one."

"Maybe I don't want to be a superstar."

Molly Anne looked taken aback. "Don't say that. Of course you want to be a superstar. It's what we've been working toward for ten years."

"Yeah, well, I was practically attacked by a roving gang of women and it was scary. And you know what? I'm getting tired of this shock jock persona. I'm just pretending. It's not the real me."

"Oh please, everyone is pretending to be something they're not. It's the way the world works," Molly Anne whispered and dragged her over to meet the reporter.

"Callie meet Brooke Burnett from *Celebrity Insider*. Brooke, this is Callie Ryder, the hippest sex guru ever to hit the airwaves."

Callie mentally groaned. *Celebrity Insider* had a reputation for stirring up both controversy and idle gossip. What had Molly Anne been thinking when lining up this particular entertainment show for an interview? But she already knew the answer. In Molly Anne's opinion any publicity was good publicity. Her friend lived and died by that motto. And Callie had to admit that without Molly Anne's gift for public relations she would probably still be behind the mike in that dinky station in their hometown.

This your dream job, this is what you've always wanted, why are you acting so weird about the attention? Trust Molly Anne. She's rarely steered you wrong.

"Hello, Callie," the perky reporter greeted. "We won't take up much of your time. We know you're a busy woman. We have just a few questions. Mostly about your book tour."

Callie forced a smile. "Sure, Brooke. I'm flattered to be interviewed by the *Celebrity Insider*."

The camera crew set up and started filming. Brooke did a short intro about catching up with rising star, Manhattan shock jock Callie Ryder, at LAX just as she was beginning the first leg of her whirlwind West Coast book tour in Los Angeles. A crowd was gathering but Callie was barely cognizant of passersby. Mostly, she was aware of the hard knot of anxiety eating at her stomach.

On the radio she was cool, calm, slick and urbane. When she slipped into her on-air persona, the real Callie became anonymous as she lost herself in the part. But here, in the airport, in person, on camera, on television, well it was different.

She'd had no time to brace herself. No warning. No warm-up. No catching her breath. She shot Molly Anne an I'm-going-to-get-even-with-you-for-this-one look.

"So tell us, Callie," Brooke said, thrusting the microphone under her nose. "If you're such a great sexpert, how come you're twenty-eight years old and you've never been in a committed relationship? Why should any young woman looking for love take advice from you?"

"Uh…I…" Callie blinked, blindsided by the question. She'd never claimed to have the secret to a long-term relationship. Her message for women was about enjoying your sexuality, not how to get married and set up housekeeping. She was just about to say as much, when a woman in the crowd spoke up.

"Hey, Brooke, do your research before you waylay people."

"Pardon me?" It was Brooke's turn to look blindsided.

"Callie's in a committed relationship right this very minute," another voice chimed in. "We met her fella and he's one wicked hottie. You can tell from the way they look at each other that they're madly in love."

Huh? Callie turned around to see the Tulane sorority sisters sticking up for her.

Great. Terrific. With fans like these two, who needed detractors?

Brooke motioned for the camera crew to stop filming and turned to Callie. "Is this true?"

The reporter looked visibly disappointed. Her eyes said it all. If Callie was indeed in a committed relationship, her muckraking ambush had gone seriously awry.

"Yes," Molly Anne quickly interjected before Callie

had time to deny the notion. "In fact, Callie and Luke are engaged."

Excuse me? Openmouthed, Callie spun around to stare at her oldest friend.

But she just stood there, stunned. For once Molly Anne had shocked her and not the other way around. But how could she confront her friend in front of the reporter?

"So where is this paragon?" Brooke asked, wrinkling her nose as if she smelled a rat.

"Uh…" Callie detested lying but she had no clue how to get out of this. She gestured vaguely. "He's around here somewhere."

"Well then." Brooke gave an evil smile. "Go get your fiancé so we can congratulate him."

"He's shy," Callie said.

"Oh, I'm sure you can persuade him to come over and say hi to the cameras for the sake of your career." Brooke stared Callie down, daring her to deny she had a fiancé.

Dammit. The smart-aleck reporter had screwed her to the wall and she couldn't let the smug woman win this battle of wills. There was no way around it. She would have to get Luke back.

"LET ME GET THIS STRAIGHT. You not only want to rehire me as Callie's bodyguard but you also want me to pretend to be her fiancé?"

Luke glared at Molly Anne Armstrong. He couldn't believe what the woman was asking and he wasn't about to agree to it. He, Callie and Molly Anne were grouped at the ticket counter while some Hollywood television reporter and her camera crew waited just a few yards away.

"That's correct." Molly Anne nodded. "It's vitally important to Callie's career."

"I'm sorry," he said. "No. I won't do it. I don't lie. I'm not a liar."

"Not even if we double your fee?" Molly Anne tempted him.

Luke hesitated for the briefest of moments. The extra money would go a long way to stabilizing the family security firm's finances. But he simply could not accept the conditions. He was an honorable man and honorable men did not lie without a damned good excuse. And salvaging Callie Ryder's attractive fanny from a fire of her own making was not nearly good enough.

"What!" Callie glared at her business manager. "What are you suggesting Molly Anne? Doubling the Incredible Hulk's salary just to have him pretend to be my fiancé. This is an insult."

Luke gave Callie a quick once-over and he realized Molly Anne was springing this on her for the first time and she was just as incensed as he by the suggestion. At least they agreed on something.

"I've just okayed the additional expenditure with Roger," Molly Anne said. "He realizes getting exposure on *Celebrity Insider* will bring a lot of attention to KSXX and he's agreed to pony up the extra cash if Luke will agree to stay."

"I'd rather be engaged to a polar bear," Callie said. "He'd be a lot more fun. Can't we just hire some guy off the street?"

"I'm sorry," Luke reiterated, jerking a thumb at Callie. "There is not enough money in the world for me to lie about being engaged to *her*. So if you ladies would excuse me, the next plane bound for home leaves in less than an hour and there's a backlog of passengers at the security checkpoint."

"Mr. Cardasian," Molly Anne started in again, a wheedling tone in her voice. "Luke. What's it going to take to persuade you to stay?"

"Nothing could persuade me to stay, Ms. Armstrong," he said firmly. "I'm not interested."

"All right." Molly Anne's tone turned frosty. "If you refuse to help us, then I must insist you pay back the retainer KSXX has already given your brother."

"Of course," Luke said, fully realizing he was going to have to borrow the money in order to repay it. But it would be worth the hassle and expense of taking out a loan if it meant shedding these crazy women once and for all. "I'll have the money to you within ten business days."

"I'll need payment immediately." Molly Anne extended her palm. "I will accept a check." Who would have thought the wan blonde could be so hard-nosed? Luke barely hung on to his temper.

"Let him go," Callie said. "You can't blackmail the guy into staying."

"Cal…" Molly Anne started to argue, but Callie held up a hand to silence her.

"Mr. Cardasian has every right to be upset with me. I did violate his orders and slipped off without his permission. I'll pay for his retainer out of my own pocket."

"I don't want your charity," Luke said.

"It's not charity. You've put up with a great deal from me," Callie said. "You deserve the fee."

For a minute there he really thought she meant it, that her contrition was genuine. But then he reminded himself she was in the entertainment industry and most of those people would do anything to further their careers even if it meant pretending to be something they weren't.

He searched her eyes. She met his gaze. She didn't shift or blink or look away. Oh, she was good. He had grossly underestimated her. She was much more than a pretty face with a sexy body. The lady was a worthy opponent.

"Keep your money," Luke reiterated. "I'll pay back the retainer."

Their conversation was interrupted by a modulated, unaccented voice breaking in over the public address system. "Ms. Callie Ryder please pick up the white courtesy phone."

"You're being paged," Luke said.

"So I hear."

He didn't know why he followed her. Instinct maybe, more likely because he wanted to reiterate that he was not accepting her charity. But when she reached the courtesy phone and realized he was behind her, she motioned him away.

"Go get back in line. You'll miss your flight and neither one of us wants that."

"What are you going to do about Brooke Burnett?" He nodded at the reporter who was consulting with her camera crew.

"Not your problem."

"She might cause you some trouble."

"Personally I could care less. This is Molly Anne's

show. Let her deal with Brooke." She reached for the phone.

He could have left. He should have left. But something told him things didn't feel right. Who'd paged her? He scanned the crowd while leaning against the wall beside the phone. He didn't see anything suspicious, but he couldn't shake the nagging sensation that something was amiss. He would wait until she got off the phone. Just to make sure everything was okay and then he would be on his way.

You already quit. You don't have to protect her anymore.

Problem was, he'd never quit anything in his life and it was starting to eat at him that he'd allowed this scrap of a woman to run him off the job. He flicked his gaze over at her, saw her complexion had blanched. She squeezed the receiver in a death grip.

"Callie?"

She stared at him, startled and wide-eyed. He jumped to her side, pried the receiver from her hand and lifted it to his ear.

"Hello?" he demanded. A click and then the dial tone. Luke hung up the phone and turned to look at her. He was alarmed to see her hand was shaking and even more alarmed to realize that her distress caused his own breathing to quicken.

She reacted and he reacted. Not kosher. A good bodyguard did not allow himself to react emotionally to external events. If he acted from emotion that meant he'd already lost control. And without his objectivity, he was useless to her. He tightened his jaw, hardening himself against the tender feelings battering him.

"What happened? Who was on the phone?"

She raised a hand to finger her lips and shook her head. "Him."

"The man who's been threatening you?"

"Uh-huh."

For the first time since Luke had met her, Callie appeared totally defenseless. Her vulnerability tore at him.

Stop reacting with your heart. Focus. Think. Get yourself under control.

Luke grasped her firmly yet gently. "What did the guy say?"

She gulped, raised her chin, squared her shoulders, marshalling her courage. Yes. A very good sign. The fighter in her was back.

"Let's not make a big deal of this, okay? You're leaving. I'll figure it out or get Molly Anne to hire me a new bodyguard."

He felt it then, the clutch of an unseen hook grabbing hold of his gut, digging in, twisting deep. A mortal wound. More than just his heart was in this now, his gut was reacting, too.

"What did the guy say?" Luke repeated hoarsely, still holding her soft slender shoulders pinned between his big palms.

Her eyes were dark, murky and worried. She was scared but struggling hard not to show it. "He says he's watching me."

"Right now?"

She nodded. "He described what I'm wearing. Right down to how many rings I have in my ears."

The hairs on the nape of his neck lifted. The guy *was*

dangerous. Luke let her go and pivoted on his heel to survey the terminal. He narrowed his eyes in suspicion at every male passenger in sight.

It could be any one of them. It could be the stocky man with the cell phone in line at the ticket counter. It could be the janitor pushing the floor sweeper. It could be one of Brooke Burnett's team. It could be the basketball-tall clerk at the far counter, or it could even be the harried father of three trying to corral his kids.

"What did his voice sound like?" Luke asked, still sizing up the terminal's occupants. "Did he have an accent? Did he sound old or young, or somewhere in between? Could you detect an ethnicity?"

"He was talking low, as if he was trying to disguise his voice. He's not Southern and he's probably Caucasian." Callie wrinkled her nose and Luke was heartened to see she'd stopped trembling. "But he did sound vaguely familiar. Then again I hear hundreds of voices on the radio night after night."

"You think he could be one of your regular callers?"

"Yes."

"It's not someone you know personally?"

"I couldn't say. I had difficulty hearing everything he said, he was speaking so quietly."

"Dave from Albany?"

She wrinkled her forehead. "I don't know, but I don't think so. He told me not to talk to Brooke Burnett. That if I kept my mouth shut and stopped the tour he would let me live."

Luke swore and fisted both hands. This cinched it. He couldn't walk away from Callie now, no matter how difficult it was for him to remain. She needed his protection and he'd never turned his back on someone in need.

"We can't let this guy win," he said.

"We?" She met his eyes. "I thought you were going back to New York."

"And let that jerk get away with terrorizing you? Not on your life." Was it his imagination or did she look relieved that he was staying?

"So what are we going to do?"

"Follow my lead."

"I'm not a follower."

"A man just threatened your life. Don't you think it's time you listened to someone else for a change?"

She thought about it for a moment. "What are you intending?"

"On becoming your fiancé."

Without another word, Luke put a hand to her back and swiveled her toward the camera crew. Once he was sure they had Brooke Burnett's undivided attention, he tilted Callie's chin up, lowered his head and kissed her.

5

ALL THE AIR FLED Callie's lungs and Luke inhaled it.

Inhaled her.

She was so stunned she couldn't think. Her mind was spinning in a thousand different directions. Why was this staid, straitlaced bodyguard suddenly kissing her?

She liked it, though. She liked it a lot.

His demanding lips took possession of hers. Callie's natural impulse was to push Luke away, to deny the powerful pull. His lips scared her that much.

But the wild, wicked side she spent so many years cultivating could not resist the temptation. The Midnight Ryder who whispered suggestive sex tips every night on the radio wasn't about to wrench her mouth from his. Not when he was kissing her like this.

On the contrary, the Midnight Ryder wanted nothing more than to grab him by the collar, lead him off to some darkened recess and jump his handsome bones. Captured in his embrace, Callie felt her entire body grow warm. She felt as if she was sliding, melting. Her senses yearned for what his lips promised.

Sex and lots of it.

Her pulse fluttered. Her surroundings, including the curious onlookers, were forgotten as she was swept into the taste of him.

She felt the sharp poke of his erection pressing hard against her thigh and a thrust of dizziness nearly took her knees out from under her. He was long, thick and hard, no secrets on that score. Those extra large condoms would most certainly be a nice fit. She thought of them both naked. Imagined him inside her, filling her up.

Her fingers curled around his bicep and she clung to him, afraid if she let go she would stumble and fall.

He was at once volatile and steady. His inner core unshakable. She could feel it in the calm way his hands held her. But his mouth was an inferno, explosive, hazardous, unstoppable.

His paradox appealed to Callie. For a lot of years, she'd acted one way on the outside, feeling another on the inside. She understood what it was like to have two masters driving you in opposite directions at once.

Hold back.

Plunge ahead.

Caution. Slow down.

Go, go, go.

He bit her gently and she almost yelped. Not because he'd hurt her, but because his boldness took her by surprise. Had she ever in her life been this turned on?

If she had, she couldn't remember when. And that was saying something considering the suggestive nature of her job, Callie got turned on quite often.

His mouth was alive, kissing, nibbling, suckling her in a way only a devoted lover could. He wanted her. That much was clear. Yet at the center of his desire, she sensed hesitation. His body ached for hers, but his stubborn mind still resisted.

She opened her eyes and saw he was peering down at her. She boldly met his gaze, challenging him, daring him to back away. *Come on, you started this. Finish what you began, soldier.*

That did it.

His pride and his lust won out. He was a man after all and he'd been too long without this. She could taste the urgency on his tongue, feel it transfer through his very skin from him to her and she caught the fever.

More, more.

She drank him in. His essence like the richest, rarest liquid on earth. She would have some kind of fodder for her radio show when this tour was over. New topic of discussion—let's see, the sensuous power of public displays of affection maybe?

Nah. Too wordy. She'd need something snappier, shorter, more…

But she never got to finish the thought because his tongue was stroking the inside of her mouth so provocatively her brain went numb. She was unaware of anything except the glorious sensation. If he could do this to her with nothing but a kiss, what would happen if she coaxed him into bed?

What a sizzling seduction that would be.

A seduction. Yes, exactly. That was what she needed to while away the time on the book tour. Bring Sir Galahad to his knees. And if his rock-hard erection was any indication, the man could do with a good orgasm or two himself.

She moaned softly into his mouth, frustrated they could not take this further. Luke took her hands and curled her into him without breaking their connection. She nestled her body against his, relishing the fact that she could make him so hard. She moved her hips in a carnal motion, promising him so much more.

He slipped his tongue deeper inside her mouth and she felt the world fall away. Callie supposed they might have gone on kissing forever if Molly Anne, Brooke Burnett, her camera crew and a handful of the sorority sisters hadn't finally converged upon them, demanding to know all the details of their torrid affair.

Whoa!

Callie grinned as the limo they'd taken from LAX pulled up in the circular driveway of the resort hotel perched on a cliff overlooking the Pacific Ocean. The grounds were awash with colorful flowers in full bloom. The verdant lawn was immaculately manicured. Expensive cars sat in the parking lot and a valet waited at the ready for them to alight from their limo.

Very romantic.

At the bottom of the road that had led up to the cliff, sat the bookstore where Callie's first signing was scheduled for the following evening. Not far away from the bookstore lay Madigan's, a trendy meet-n-greet bar. Molly Anne had reserved the private dining room for a big, blowout reception after the signing to celebrate the start of Callie's tour.

Callie had seen the guest list. It included many movers and shakers in the West Coast publishing world, but until that moment it hadn't really hit her that she would be rubbing elbows with Hollywood glitterati. She swallowed, unable to absorb it all.

Her most fervent dreams were coming true. So why did she feel more overwhelmed than elated? Why did she have an intense desire to scuttle back to New York as fast as her legs would carry her?

Slip into Midnight Ryder mode. Think outrageous. That ought to get you in the swing of things.

Luke was sitting beside her, sunglasses on, face impassive, mood undecipherable. She poked him in the ribs with her elbow.

"Check it out." She nodded at the thick shrubbery circling the front of the resort. "A girl could slip off with her favorite guy for a quickie behind the hedgerow and no one would ever be the wiser."

"Except for the gardener," he shot back.

"Well," she teased, "the chance of getting caught is half the fun of doing it in a public place."

"You ever made love in a public place?"

"Dozens of times." She waved two fingers with a flourish. "You?"

"No." He turned his face away from her. To hide a smile? More likely he was cloaking a blush.

Callie's grin widened. Luke was so easy to fluster when it came to sex. The man was ripe for seduction whether he would admit it or not. The poor guy had been too long without. She could see it in the lean and hungry expression that tightened his mouth and clung over his shoulders whenever he looked at her in *that* way.

Sir Galahad, the chaste, was in desperate need of corrupting.

And this easy, breezy resort was exactly the place to get started. Because if she was busy seducing her bodyguard, she could forget how nervous she was about this whole trip and what it meant for her future.

A future she wanted and yet, did not. Little wonder she was a Gemini. Mercurial, impulsive, occasionally moody, adept at covering up her insecurities with a well-executed act.

Molly Anne entered the resort ahead of them.

Luke had his arm around Callie's waist, solicitous as any good pretend fiancé should be. His possessiveness bugged her but at the same time she also loved it. What was the matter with her? Where were all these conflicting feelings coming from?

He brushed against her side and she felt the hardness of his handgun underneath his coat. The weapon startled her. She knew he had a gun. He had to check it with airport security for the flight. But until now she hadn't realized how serious this stalker business really was. His gun caused her to consider that she might actually be in danger.

Callie thought again of the voice on the phone, threatening her to keep her mouth shut. The man had sounded vaguely familiar but she could not place his voice. He must have been one of the callers on her show. It was the only thing she could come up with.

Even now, after this latest threat, she was reluctant

to consider the man really meant her harm. He was just a crackpot who didn't like her feminist views on sex. That was all.

So why had he gone to the trouble of tracking her down at LAX? Her heart skipped a beat, but she denied her fear, pushing it down deep inside. She would not give in to it.

"Is that a gun in your pocket or are you just happy to see me?" she flirted, more as a means to distract herself than anything else. She already employed this defense mechanism with him. Using his kiss in the airport to drown out her fears. Since the technique had worked to keep her mind off the stalker then, why not keep using it?

"Hush," Luke growled.

"Getting all businesslike on me?" she asked, trying to lighten the mood, except by-the-book Luke wasn't exactly a lighthearted guy.

"I'm observing the bystanders," he said. "Doing my job. Watching people for signs of trouble."

Callie shivered. Not from fear of the menace, but from the dangerous look in Luke's eyes as he removed his sunglasses and studied her intently.

Wowza, okay, let's move on.

Molly Anne went to the front desk to check them in. The bellboy followed with their luggage.

"Let's stop off at the gift shop," Luke said.

"Why," she teased. "Stocking up on more condoms?" Oh, she was bad and she knew it, but where was the fun in being good?

"Ha, ha."

"Hey, we could easily go through a box of condoms. You are supposed to be my fiancé."

"Not my idea."

"Not mine, either, but you're here and I'm just having fun yanking your chain."

"Being your fiancé is just my cover. It's nothing more than doing my job."

"Coulda fooled me. That kiss at the airport didn't feel particularly dutiful."

He ignored the comment and guided her into the gift shop, his eyes narrowing as he took in the lanky teen behind the counter. "Got any hair dye?"

"For you or for her?" the young man asked, giving Callie an appreciative once-over.

Hair dye? What was he getting at?

"Her." Luke jerked a thumb in her direction.

"Yep. In the cosmetic section. Not a huge selection, though."

"I am not changing my hair color," Callie protested.

"You stick out like a lit match with that purply-pink hair," Luke said. "You're switching to a normal color for your own safety."

He was making her mad again. Priggishness was one thing. If he wanted to act as though he had a bug up his backside that was his business. But demanding that she alter her hair color was another thing entirely.

She lowered her voice but had to stand on tiptoes to reach his ear. The guy should come equipped with a stepladder. "You were hired to protect me, not critique my choice of hair color," she hissed.

"I *am* protecting you. That's the point. To keep you from drawing so much attention to yourself. It'll make my job a lot easier if you blend in with the general populace."

"I like attention." She tossed her head.

"Would never have guessed."

"You're her, aren't you?" the clerk asked. "That lady deejay. I've caught your show a couple of times. We just started getting it here. I recognized you from your picture on the poster in the bookstore down the street."

"Yep. That's me."

"I agree with you." The clerk nodded. "I like your hair the way it is. Sweet. Very L.A."

"Thank you." She smiled smugly at Luke.

"He didn't mean 'sweet' like naive and innocent, did he?" Luke whispered.

"No, it means cool. As in hip, with it, happening."

"That's what I thought."

"Um…" The clerk hesitated. "Do you think maybe I could get an autograph? Would you mind?"

"I'd be happy to give you an autograph." Callie stepped away from Luke's overprotective grasp.

"Here, sign this." The clerk pulled a piece of paper from a spiral notebook under the counter and thrust it toward her along with a pen. "Could you say something outrageous. You know, like *To Justin, thanks for the best sex of my life.*"

"No she cannot." Luke snatched the paper from Callie and crumpled it tight in his fist. "She's my fiancée and she is not going to sign smut for some snot-nosed punk."

Woo. Hold the phone. What was that all about? Callie stared at Luke, surprised by his outburst.

"Dude, no offense." The young guy held up his palms. "But when you've got a lady as hot as the Midnight Ryder, you gotta expect some competition."

"Hair dye." Luke gritted out the words and loomed menacingly over the counter. "What aisle?"

The clerk pointed.

Luke marched over, grabbed a bottle of Miss Clairol off the shelf and brought it back to the counter. "Ring this up."

"What color is it?" Callie asked, trying to get a glimpse at the box. "I don't like subtle shades."

He peeled open his wallet and handed the clerk enough money to cover the purchase. Then he picked up the sack, snatched Callie by the hand and dragged her out of the gift shop.

Molly Anne met them in the lobby waving plastic key cards and grinning as if she was up to something.

"What is it?" Callie asked, recognizing the look on her friend's face. Usually that overly enthusiastic expression meant Molly Anne had cooked up an idea she feared Callie wasn't going to approve.

"I changed your reservations and booked you guys into the honeymoon suite," Molly Anne said.

"Are you out of your mind?"

It was bad enough that Luke was already living in her back pocket. The last thing they needed was to share a romantic boudoir. She would end up chasing him around the bedroom like Pepé Le Pew and Luke would be resisting like the poor little black cartoon kitty with the white paint down her back. Except unlike starry-eyed Pepé, it wasn't love Callie wanted, but sex.

"Hear me out." Molly Anne raised both palms while at the same time lowering her voice in a conspiratorial tone. "I'm leaking a rumor that you guys have secretly eloped. Brilliant huh?"

Lori Wilde

"More like brain dead," Callie protested. "What were you thinking? This trip is supposed to be about the book tour, not about titillating paparazzi with my imaginary love life."

"You don't get it, do you?" Molly Anne shook her head over Callie's apparent denseness. "This trip *is* about selling books. And the best way I know how to do that is to stir up interest in your personal life. There's nothing your fans would want to hear more than that you've found love."

"But isn't love the antithesis of my image?"

Molly Anne waved a hand. "Yes, but people still eat that stuff up."

"But I haven't found love. Luke's not my fiancé. We're not eloping. This has nothing to do with my job as a deejay." Callie knew she was whining but she did not want to do this thing.

"Oh, that's where you're wrong. It has everything to do with it. Do you want to reach for the stars or not?" Molly Anne frowned, cocked one hand on her hip and pointed a finger at her.

"Honestly?" Callie said. "If I have to keep making up stories and pretending to be someone I'm not, then maybe I don't want stardom."

"You're never satisfied with anything I do for you. You're always thinking there's something better around the next bend. That's why you've never been in love. That's why you don't have a *real* fiancé."

"I don't have a fiancé because I don't want one. Besides, you don't have a man, either," Callie challenged.

"That's because I'm too busy looking after your career. And while you might not want stardom—" Molly Anne started to shout but realized they were in a public place, caught herself and lowered her voice to whisper fiercely. "I do."

"Fine, great, go get your own radio show and stop living vicariously through me." Callie blew out her breath and braced herself. This showdown with Molly Anne was long overdue. The more her friend pushed her, the more Callie felt lost in her own skin.

"I can't believe you said that to me." Molly Anne's lip quivered and she looked as if Callie had just struck her across the face. "After everything we've been through together."

Aw hell.

Callie immediately felt contrite. She hadn't intended on hurting her friend's feelings. They had been through a lot together. Unhappy childhoods, the death of Molly Anne's father, Callie's pregnancy scare her senior year in high school. They had shared laughter and tears, adventures and problems. At times their personalities had clashed. Meticulous Molly Anne and Chaotic Callie, the female odd couple.

They'd been poor together, living on generic brand diet cola and baked potatoes both in college and those lean years afterward. And now, thanks to Molly Anne's business acumen, they were finally starting to get rich together.

"I'm sorry," Callie apologized. "That comment was uncalled for."

"It's okay." Molly Anne turned her head away.

"No it's not. It was a mean thing to say. Please forgive me. I'm just overwhelmed by all this attention. I mean, I knew I was making inroads in New York. But I had no idea I was causing a sensation across the country. And it is all thanks to you."

"Apology accepted." Molly Anne smiled past the mist of tears gathering in the corners of her eyes.

Callie held open her arms and they embraced, squeezing each other tight. She didn't want to destroy an eighteen-year friendship over something as insignificant as Molly Anne reserving the honeymoon suite without asking her first.

"All is forgiven?"

"All is forgiven," Molly Anne echoed. Her eyes brightened. She waved the key cards. "Now you two go check out that swanky honeymoon suite."

6

LUKE PLUCKED THE KEY CARD from Callie's hand, insisting on checking out the premises before letting her come inside the suite. He didn't want any nasty surprises like a mad slasher hiding in the closet.

"Stay in the hallway," he commanded, knowing full well she had a tendency to disobey him.

"What if someone attacks me while you're giving the place the once-over?"

"Scream real loud." Would she ever just do what he asked without questioning his every request?

"Ha. Ha."

Ignoring her sarcasm, he searched the suite with a practiced eye, on the lookout for anything suspicious. He swept through the sitting area, not paying much attention to the decor and went on into the bedroom. He frowned when he discovered a balcony. He pulled back the draperies, flung open the French doors and stepped outside into the warm afternoon air.

The view was spectacular. The Pacific Ocean stretched out, a vivid blue jewel. Directly below was a garden ripe with colorful vegetation and intersected by a network of cobblestone walkways. A trellis of exotic-looking vines trailed up the side of the building. A breeze ruffled his hair and teased his nose with the sweet tropical scent of flowers and fruit trees.

While they might appear romantic, the balcony and French doors and vine-covered trellis were a security nightmare. Anyone so inclined could shimmy up the vines and swing over onto the balcony. It wouldn't take much to get through those French doors and into the bedroom.

Not a good situation.

If he slept on the couch in the sitting room as he had planned, an intruder could climb in through Callie's window, do her harm and Luke might never hear it. He realized that whether he liked the idea or not, he was going to have to sleep in the bedroom with her.

But he would sleep on the floor, of course.

"Whoa, check this place out." Callie's voice drifted out to him. "Looks like a cotton-candy bordello."

"I told you to stay in the hallway." He stormed back inside to confront her. He was definitely going to have to stay in her room if she kept defying him. It was far more likely that Callie would sneak out the window than an intruder would sneak in.

"I got bored." She shrugged. "You were taking too long."

Luke stopped short as he finally noticed the furnishings. Holy crap.

Huge round bed covered by a red bedspread and lots of pink, heart-shaped throw pillows. Thick white carpet and mirrors. Lots and lots of mirrors. Plastered all across the ceiling.

It looked exactly like a cotton-candy bordello. He

should not look up. He knew it, but damn him, he did it anyway. Without any hindrance at all he could see right down the cleavage of Callie's low-cut blouse.

Proud, jutting, smooth and creamy—a pair of beautiful breasts. He could even make out a hint of her black lace bra.

He tilted his head, mesmerized by her lithe image. She was busy opening up the armoire to find the television set and a minibar and she hadn't noticed that he'd gone stone-cold stupid over seeing her in those mirrors. Who in their right mind could watch TV with the damn mirrors glued to the ceiling?

He tried not to stare at her, but he couldn't stop himself from admiring her long slender legs that looked so outrageous in those smokin' high-heeled sandals that matched her blood-red miniskirt. And when she bent over to peer into the minibar he was afraid he was going to pop his wad right then and there.

"Oooh, they have Godiva chocolates. My favorite. So sinfully delicious they ought to be against the law." Her tight skirt stretched provocatively across her fanny.

Luke gulped. A shaft of heat caught fire in his throat and blazed all the way down to his groin. Close your eyes. Stop ogling her.

But he could not.

Callie straightened and turned toward him, a chocolate truffle in one hand. "I've heard good chocolate is an aphrodisiac. Should we put it to the test and see if the rumor is true?"

"The hotel probably charges twenty-five dollars a chocolate."

"Maybe that's the aphrodisiac part. Spending a decadent fortune on them."

"Put the chocolates away."

Callie angled a glance toward the ceiling and met his gaze in the overhead reflection. "Oh, food isn't what does it for you, huh? You're more into watching?"

"No, no," Luke denied, vigorously shaking his head. That last thing he wanted was to get her going on one of her sexy riffs. "I'm not into mirrors, either."

"That's too bad. It can be quite fun making love in front of one."

"You've done it before."

"Hasn't everyone?"

Um, no.

She must have seen the truth on his face, because she licked her lips and winked saucily. She knew exactly what she was doing. "I'm getting the feeling you're just a tad uptight when it comes to sex."

"I'm not uptight about sex," he said.

"No? Then let's see how soft the bed is," she suggested and proceeded to jump onto the circular monstrosity, coming down in the middle with both knees. Her skirt kicked up a bit in the back as she did so, giving him a fantastic glimpse of her panties.

She was wearing a G-string thong.

A black one.

Luke sucked in his breath. The sound was clearly audible in the room. He felt as if he'd been punched solidly in the diaphragm.

Callie glanced at him over her shoulder, her look pure

coy, pinup queen. The minx. She bounced on the mattress a couple of times. "Cushy. Wanna give it a try?"

"Stop that," he insisted.

"Stop what?"

"Trying to seduce me."

"But why? You can't deny it. We've got chemistry together. The sexual current is so strong you could snap it like a rubber band, and if you're not uptight about sex as you claim..." She let the thought trail off.

"I'm not denying I want you so badly I can taste it. Which is why you must stop provoking me."

She popped an index finger into her mouth, slowly moving it in and out as she sucked on it.

"So go ahead," she said, and extended her slick, wet finger toward him. "Taste it."

He shook his head. In his mind, that finger was already in his mouth.

"Why not?" she repeated.

"I'm your bodyguard," Luke said, his objections sounding feeble even to his own ears.

"And?"

"A sexual relationship with you would compromise my objectivity."

"Shh." Again, she lifted that naughty finger to her lips. "I won't tell if you won't."

"Callie..."

"What?"

"I'm not going to make love to you."

"Okay."

"You're giving up that easily?" He didn't believe it

for a minute and he eyed her suspiciously, trying to figure out what was going on in that head of hers.

"Sure. If you're not interested, you're not interested. I understand." She shrugged. How could she be so blasé about having her sexual advances rejected?

"I am interested," he said through clenched teeth. "So interested I can't think rationally. And that's the problem."

"Come here," she whispered.

"I'm fine right where I am." He crossed his arms over his chest and tried to look rigid and strong but his knees were so weak he feared they'd buckle if he had to walk too far.

She crooked her wet index finger, smiled and repeated in her cajoling, singsongy Southern accent, "Come 'ere, honey."

"What is it?"

She didn't answer, just kept smiling and crooking her finger. Shoot. Reluctantly, he ambled over.

"Sit." She patted a spot beside her on the bed.

Luke slowly blew out a breath and perched next to her, his body tensed, legs ready to spring to a standing position at the first signs of groping.

"Relax." She reached over to loosen his tie and he stiffened beneath her touch. "Take off that suit and tie and let me give you a shoulder rub."

"I don't need a shoulder rub." He angled his body away from hers.

"You're so tense your neck muscles are straining against your collar."

"I like being tense."

"So I've noticed."

Without warning, she leaned over and quickly flicked the tip of her hot wet tongue around the outer rim of his ear. Luke shuddered, imagining what else she might do. "Please," he said, upset to hear that he was begging. "Stop trying to seduce me."

"We're going to be sharing a room for three weeks, Luke, it's bound to happen eventually. You feel it, I feel it. Why not start now and we can have three weeks of fun, fun, fun."

"Because I'm not a 'fun' kind of guy."

"Well, I kinda already figured that out, but you are a man and I'm a woman and we're both young and healthy and there's nothing wrong with scratching an itch as long as you protect yourself."

"I didn't say there was anything wrong with it, I just said I can't." He jumped to his feet and shoved a hand through his hair. He looked everywhere but at her. If he met her gaze, he knew he would be a goner because all he could think about was kissing her again the way he had kissed her at the airport. "It's nothing personal. I think you're an exciting woman and damned sexy...."

"But?"

He sighed, ran a palm down the side of his face. "I don't believe in casual sex."

"Is premarital sex against your religion or something?"

"It's not that."

"What is it then?"

He shrugged, embarrassed. He knew his views on sex and love ran counterclockwise to most people. "I want sex to be special. You know, emotionally as well as physically."

"You don't mean sex, you're talking about making love."

"Yes."

"You're an odd duck, you know that?"

"So I've been told."

"With you it's true love or nothing?"

"That's about the size of it."

Her eyes danced. "Oh I hope it's much bigger than that."

"Stop being suggestive."

"Aw, you're no fun." She scooted around to prop herself up against the pillows and cross her legs to sit tailor style on the red satin bedspread. "I've got a question, but you don't have to answer if you don't want to."

"Fire away."

"Are you a virgin, Luke?"

"I'm closing in on thirty." He snorted. "What do you think?"

"I'm thinking you are."

"I've had sex."

"How many times?"

"A few," he mumbled.

"With how many partners?"

"More than one," he said defensively.

"That means two?"

"Yes. I've had sex with only two women. I suppose you think I'm a freak of nature." Why was he telling her this? She and that rich drawl had a way of making a man spill his guts, even when he didn't want to.

"Let me guess. You fell madly in love with the first woman. You thought she loved you as much as you loved her. Then she cheated on you and you got your heart broke and then with the second gal you had trouble letting down your guard."

He jerked his head, not really nodding, but sort of. How could he tell her the truth about Rachel Delong? He'd gotten his heart broken all right, but it wasn't for the reason Callie guessed.

"We were kids. Barely seventeen. Rachel's betrayal hurt at the time. But I got over it."

"Did you?"

"Yes."

"So what happened with the second woman?"

He worked his jaw, not wanting to discuss it.

"Well?" Callie prodded.

"Elysse said she needed someone more adventuresome in bed."

"So why not become more adventuresome?"

"I tried but the problems between us were deeper than that and she didn't want to work on them."

"Why haven't you moved on since then?"

"I haven't found anyone who interested me," Luke said. *Until you.* "Plus I was out of the country for six years and I didn't want to start a relationship that had no future."

"But you're back home now. It's time to dust yourself off, move on."

"It's easier for some people than others," he said gloomily.

"Are you still in love with the first woman?"

"Hell no," he said sharply. He'd never been in love with Rachel. That had been the problem. They'd just been two kids fooling around without any clue about the consequences of what they were messing with.

"Then there's only one surefire cure."

"I don't need a cure. I'm fine."

"You haven't had sex in six years? With a partner I mean. I'm sure you've found other ways to release the sexual tension." She smiled and wriggled her eyebrows.

He had to clench his jaw to keep from blushing. Dammit. Why did he have to embarrass so easily? He wished he could stop sneaking peeks at her. Wished she wasn't so magnetic with her crooked smile and her fuchsia hair and all that jingly jewelry.

"You're just scared to begin again."

"Yeah," he reluctantly admitted. "Maybe that's part of it."

She clicked her tongue and gave a soft sigh. "Ah, honey, that's so sad."

The way she said *honey* made him feel sad. And prudish and hung up and foolish.

"You've missed out on a lot," she noted.

"I'm sure I have."

"We could have such a good time together. You and I. If you'd relax your expectations about love and sex."

"No doubt."

She lowered her voice. "Come on, Luke, tell me the truth. What are you really afraid of?"

"Afraid? I'm not afraid."

But even as he denied it, he felt it. Deep inside his chest, pushing hard against his heart. His longing for something precious and perfect that he feared might not even exist.

What *was* he so damned afraid of?

He shook his head. He did not want to examine the question. He wasn't afraid of anything. He was frustrated, that was all. And mad at himself because he wanted something he shouldn't have. Like a diabetic sneaking birthday cake.

And that's all a tryst with Callie would ever be. Birthday cake.

It might be delicious and sweet and those first few bites, pure heaven. But later, the guilt would set in and the sugar rush would be gone, and what would he be left with?

"I'm sorry," he repeated. "I can't make love to you, Callie. For your own good as much as mine."

CALLIE WANTED LUKE and she wasn't giving up so easily.

He was the opportunity she'd been waiting for all her life. An inexperienced but potent lover. A man she could mold in bed. How fun it would be to school him in the erogenous arts. He was smart and sexy and if she could get him over his inhibitions she knew he would be dynamite.

But it would be a tricky proposition. He did possess a stunning measure of self-control. Fortunately, she thrived on challenges and she adored acting on impulse.

"I think I'll take a shower," she said. "Wash off the road grime."

"Might be time to color your hair, too," he suggested.

"You're still insisting on that?"

"It's for your own safety."

"Yeah, yeah." She swung her legs off the bed, got to her feet, casually stripped her blouse over her head and tossed it on t bed beside Luke. Her pulse raced with anticipation. What would he do when he saw her standing in nothing but her bra and panties?

"What are you doing?!" He sounded horrified and panicky and turned on all at the same time.

Big score for Callie.

She dipped her head so he couldn't see her triumphant smile.

"Getting undressed." She shimmied her skirt past her hips and then let it drop to her feet.

"Um…um…er," Luke mumbled, clearly desperate for any excuse to escape. "I better give you some privacy."

"Stay. I don't mind." She reached around for the hook at the back of her bra.

"Why are you torturing me like this?" he croaked.

"Because I'm wicked to the core." She stuck her tongue out at him and laughed. She unhooked the bra, but left it dangling in place, the straps draped loosely over her shoulders.

He studied her for a long moment, his eyes inscrutable, but his breathing gave him away. He was almost panting.

They stared at each other.

Endlessly.

Callie realized she, too, was breathing hard and heavy.

"You're not wicked," he said finally.

"How do you know?"

"You're just trying to shock me."

"I'm not. I'm trying to get you into bed."

"By shocking me."

She conceded his point with a slight smile and a tilt of her head. "Foreplay."

"I've got you figured out." He bobbed a finger at her.

"Oh? How's that?"

"You're hiding your true self behind the outrageousness."

"I'm not," she bluffed but she was blindsided by a rush of emotions that made her want to laugh and cry at the same time. Nervousness, excitement, a strange thrill at the idea that at last, here was someone who "got" her.

Where had this feeling come from?

Where had he come from?

Suddenly, she was aware that she was almost naked in front of him and she had to force herself not to pick up her clothes and cloak herself with them. How had he managed to quickly turn the tables on her? One minute she was in control and the next, she was figuratively on her back, pinned to the mat by the soft expression of understanding in his eyes.

Help!

Immediately, she denied what she was feeling, and let her bra drop to the floor. His gaze welded to her breasts and his eyes widened. That's when Callie knew she was in control again.

"I'll just be in the shower if you decide you'd like to join me."

"Thanks for the invitation. But I've got a lot to do."

"Uh-huh. Right, chicken," she said.

He turned and almost ran into the sitting area, closing the door securely behind him.

To shut her in?

Or to keep himself out?

She was getting to him. No doubt about it. There was just one thing left to do if she hoped to help poor Sir Galahad find his way home to come-a-lot.

Turn up the heat!

Because the poor man needed casual, lighthearted sex almost as much as he needed to breathe.

7

"Yew-hoo, Luke."

Five minutes later, he thought he heard Callie calling to him from the bathroom over the sound of running water. He cocked his head and listened. He was perched on the edge of the couch, his heart shoving blood through his veins at an alarming clip. At one point back there in the bedroom, he had come within inches of ripping off his clothes and taking Callie in a hard, hot rush.

The woman tested him in unanticipated ways. And he'd never expected himself to come up so short. She called to a part of himself he'd turned his back on a long time ago. The playful kid that had been lost forever at seventeen. But his feelings for her were more primal. She stirred in him a need he hadn't known existed. She challenged him to seek a new reality for himself, to let go of the past and make himself over. A fresh start. A new beginning. A different outlook.

And let's face it, there was the sexual angle. He had never experienced anything like the thrill he got watching Callie strip off her clothes.

She wanted him to crack. But he would not.

Could not.

Could he?

He heard the water turn off.

"Oh, Luke, could you please come in here a sec?"

Nothing doing. Absolutely not. No way was he going into that bathroom with her.

"Luke!" Her voice took on an anxious quality. "I need you."

He swallowed. What if she really was in trouble and not just trying to seduce him? But what could have happened to her in the bathroom? He fisted his hands against his knees trying to decide what to do.

You're her bodyguard, you can't ignore her cry for help.

"Please come in here, I'm in something of a fix."

Aw hell, like it or not he was going to have to go into that bathroom. Putting on his game face, he got up and went into the bedroom. The bathroom door stood ajar.

"What is it?" he asked.

"I'm hung up."

"Hung up?"

"Just come in here," she said.

"If this is just another one of your ploys to embarrass me I'm going to be mad."

"It's not, I swear."

He hesitated a moment, then resolutely toed the door open farther. He stuck his head into the bathroom.

Callie sat in the middle of an oversize hot tub filled with lavender-scented bubbles. Her back was to him and she was surrounded in a steamy fog. She was leaning over and the first thing he fixed on was the sumptuous curve of her spine. She had one hand resting on top of her head, thick with shampoo lather. That was when he saw that one of her bracelets had become entangled with her hair.

Just looking at her made Luke's pulse jump. There were bubbles dribbling down her neck, drawing his eyes to her slender shoulder blade and glistening golden skin.

God, she was gorgeous. He felt himself grow instantly hard.

She turned her head and met his gaze. "Thank heavens. I thought you were going to be too damned stubborn to come in."

"I'm here," he said gruffly.

"So untangle me already," she said, lifting her wrist as high as it would go above her head.

Luke gulped, braced himself to handle the situation and trod across the floor toward her.

"This is all your fault," she said as he pushed her hair-care supplies to one side and sat down on the tub.

"How so?"

"You were the one who insisted I color my hair."

"I didn't tell you to wear bracelets while you were doing it. Lean over so I can get at you better."

"Oooh," she teased. "I like the sound of that."

She leaned into him, dampening his shirt as she rested her head on his thigh. Her warm breath spread across his skin, raising gooseflesh up his arms. He tried not to think about how great it felt to have her nestled against him, or how easy it would be to surrender to temptation and have sex with her right there in the tub.

His gaze slid down and he caught himself peeking at the smooth hollow underneath her raised arm. The sight of her armpit shouldn't have been sexy or seductive, but it was.

His fingers worked at the clasp of her bracelet. It would be easier to detach it from her hair once her wrist was freed.

Callie pushed a tendril of loose hair from her face and peered up at him. There was no mistaking the appreciation in her eyes as she visually caressed his face. That and the slight groan that slipped from her lips let him know how much she was enjoying this.

Luke felt self-conscious. He wasn't accustomed to being in the bath with gorgeous naked women. Especially a woman who'd clearly voiced her desire for him. It had been so long since he'd touched soft feminine flesh so intimately.

Too damned long.

However, it wasn't the time or the place, nor was Callie the right woman to be breaking his celibacy over.

But God, how he wanted to.

He pretended to fiddle with the bracelet but instead, he was trying not to panic at the feel of her nipple hardening against the leg of his damp slacks. A corresponding hardness strained at his zipper.

Her hair was a soft and silky slide beneath his fingers. And the rhythmic rise and fall of her chest sent his own breath reeling. A heated awareness pricked his skin. He'd never felt so conscious of anything in his life.

His entire body flushed with mind-blowing heat. Damn! What was happening to him? That unabashed look in her eyes caused his pulse to jump. His hormones were flipping out.

Focus on what you're doing, Cardasian. Concentrate.

He fumbled, his fingers slipping in her wet, soapy hair, but finally, he got the bracelet undone and she was able to lower her arm.

"Thank you," she said.

"Hold still. Your hair is looped through several rings on your charms." He hoped he came off gruff and unaffected, but he was afraid he sounded hungry and needy.

Slowly, carefully, he disentangled her hair from the bracelet and set it in the soap dish.

She looked at him, her eyes bright and eager. She made him feel unique and yet he had no right to feel that way. Callie was an adventuresome woman. No doubt about it. From her mischievous grin, to her rakish smile, it was clear she appreciated sex.

And no woman had ever aroused him so intently.

She pursed her lips.

He held her gaze and then before he knew what was happening, he was kissing her. Which wasn't like him. He didn't get swept away by his desires. He was detached and introspective and restrained. It was the only way he'd survived the dangers he'd faced in Limbasa.

But his self-control was unraveling like a spool of wire rolling downhill. How was he supposed to survive three weeks on the road with Hurricane Callie?

He knew he was in trouble the instant she started kissing him back. The woman knew exactly what she was doing. The way she worked that sweet tongue of hers told him she'd had plenty of experience expressing her passion.

And he'd had very little, almost no experience.

If he hadn't followed in his father's footsteps and joined the navy. If his old childhood friend, Mukasi, hadn't asked him to come back and help guide aid workers to war-ravaged villages in Limbasa, he might be a different man today. More sophisticated, more open-minded, more accomplished in the relationship department. But he *had* joined the military and he *had* gone to Limbasa and his love life had been severely neglected because of his choices.

And he was suffering for it now.

To fight his feelings of inadequacy, he did the only thing he knew how to do well. He took control, startling Callie with the demanding pressure of his lips. Surprise flashed in her eyes and she stared him directly in the face.

He could almost read her mind. He could tell she was thinking, *I can't let him get away with this.*

She tried at that point to take over. Enfolding her slender arms around his neck and pulling him half into the tub. Fighting to maintain a position of dominance was in her nature. He had already figured that out about her, recognized the same instinct within himself. In that respect they were two of a kind, although in almost every other way they were exact opposites.

She was playful and coy and impulsive. He was taciturn and serious and precise. She was windblown. He was spit and polished. She lived to shock. He embarrassed easily. She danced to the beat of a different drummer. He marched to the tune of John Philip Sousa. She was premium ice cream and he was plain old broccoli.

And he was falling for her hard and fast.

Falling so hard he didn't mind that his clothes were wet or that his face was soapy from her kiss.

You're just horny, he told himself but Luke was afraid that wasn't the whole truth.

She kissed him, increasing the pressure, upping the tempo. Her lips blasted him into another realm of awareness, making him forget everything except the feel of her mouth under his. Her short fingernails dug into the back of his head. A deep flush of arousal painted her face, spread down her neck to her perky bosom. She was ready for action. She left no doubts about her interest.

The flick of her tongue over his teeth was lazy, sultry, teasing him by degrees. Slowly at first, but then with steadily building pressure.

She was so petite, so narrow of waist, that with his hands spread he could almost span her. God, his fingers were itching to do just that and so much more. Aching to skim every part of her, to learn all the secrets her body possessed.

"Luke," Callie moaned softly and the way she breathed his name on a sigh almost pushed him over the edge of reason.

His head spun, his heart pounded. Some bodyguard he was. He didn't even remember where they were or why they were here.

All he knew was that he had to have more.

His hand, with an amazing mind of its own, slipped down into the water to cup her tight, round bottom. His penis strained against his zipper, flourishing from sandstone to solid granite.

Flexing, he curled his fingers into the soft, willing

flesh of her buttocks. He heard her quick intake of breath and he couldn't believe what he was doing. Squeezing her so possessively.

You're out of line.

But he couldn't stop kissing her, or touching her. She was even tastier than in his fantasies. Her mouth was hot and moist and so was his. Her bottom, beneath his palm, was warm and growing hotter with each passing second. He kneaded her right where the curve of her butt met her upper thigh and she instantly trembled against him,

Ah, he'd found an erogenous zone.

The discovery pleased him inordinately. He'd never found one before and the knowledge caused him to grin.

Note to self. Don't forget this.

The air vibrated between him and Callie. Rich and hot. As rich and hot as the blood simmering through his veins.

Hell, he was in trouble here.

The erotic promise buried in that kiss made him shudder. The push of her rose-petal lips, the heat of her breath disoriented him. The form and curve of her mouth, the delightful swell of her lower lip, the sculpted bow of the upper, the edge where the textured velvet of her mouth gave way to the sultry mystery of her inner self.

At long last, she pulled away and peered at him, her eyes rounded wide.

He blinked, the spell shattered.

"Long as you're here," she said. "You might as well help me color my hair. It's tough to do a good job by yourself."

"I don't think that's such a great idea." His voice was shaky. He could tell from the expression in her eyes she heard his vulnerability.

"You're already wet," she pointed out.

His shirt was soppy, his thigh streaked with water from where she'd laid her head. "I could go get Molly Anne to help you," he offered.

"Molly Anne's allergic to a lot of chemicals."

"She could wear gloves."

"She reacts to latex, too."

"You're going to force me to do this, aren't you?"

"Pretty much."

Luke drew in a breath. He was playing with fire but he couldn't seem to make himself get up and walk out of the bathroom. "Okay then, let's get this over with."

"It'd be easier if you took off your clothes. So you don't get hair dye all over you."

"Oh, you'd like that, wouldn't you?"

"Yes I would." She grinned. That wily grin weakened his defenses and cut right to the root of his sexual longings. It was as if she knew what was in his heart and in his mind. He wanted her and for the first time in his life he hungered for a red-hot casual fling.

Scary stuff.

Unable to sort out the confusion raging in his over-sexed brain, Luke concentrated on the one thing in front of him.

Coloring Callie's hair.

She cocked her head in that coy way she had and a lock of soapy hair fell across her forehead. She arched an eyebrow expectantly. "Well? You gonna do it or not?"

Well, indeed.

Here goes nothing.

He picked up the box of hair dye and read the instructions. It did sound messy and he was wearing an expensive suit. She was right. It would be easier if he took his clothes off.

Gingerly, Luke removed his shoes, then shucked off his shirt and pants. He neatly folded his clothes and laid them on the counter. Unclothed, he sat on the ledge of the tub and stuck his legs into the bubbly water behind Callie.

She sank her head back against his shins. His muscles at first tensed and then relaxed, soothed by the water jets and silky heat. It felt as if his feet were sinking into a tub of melted chocolate. Hot, thick and sinfully delicious.

"There you go," Callie said. "Give in. Relax."

A moan of pleasure involuntarily escaped his lips as the steamy pulsations massaged his calves.

"Nice, huh?" Callie tilted back her head and grinned up at him.

He grunted. No way was he going to let her know exactly how nice it felt. He twisted the cap off the bottle of hair dye. "Let's get this over with."

Following the instructions, he applied the hair color in sections, his fingers gently massaging her scalp.

"That feels so good," she murmured.

"Hold still," he said gruffly. Touching her was making him tingle in places he had no business tingling.

She was doing this on purpose, teasing him, testing him. He would not succumb, no matter how much he might ache to give in to temptation.

"I need something to anchor me," she said and wrapped both her wrists around his ankles. "Will you be my anchor, Luke?"

He was out of his element. She knew how to flirt and he didn't. She wanted more from him than he knew how to give. He blocked that thought and kept working.

Every sensation was amplified, exaggerated—the weight of her body against his legs, the feel of her fingers tickling his anklebones, the rhythm of her breathing. The perfect shape of her head as he worked the chemically smelling solution into her silky magenta hair.

In spite of his best intentions not to get emotionally involved with Callie, she had a sneaky way of getting to him. He shouldn't be here in the tub with her. He was setting himself up for trouble.

His cock throbbed and he had to squeeze his eyes shut and clench his fists and fight for every shred of control he possessed.

She had gotten to him. She'd slipped under his radar with her sassy talk and her sex-kitten looks and that naughty crooked grin just begging him to come do wrong.

Truth was, she scared him. He'd spent so many years on constant guard, on alert, watching his every thought, his every emotion that he was stunned to learn she had sneaked her way past his defenses.

What was he going to do? If she kept tempting him, sooner or later he was going to crumble. He *was* only human.

But he valued what he valued. How could he break his own code of ethics and indulge in casual sex when he truly believed it was the road to disaster? He should know. He'd traveled down it before.

The war in Limbasa had just been an excuse. He realized that now. A place for him to take refuge. Imagine, hiding in a war-torn country.

He had convinced himself his motives were altruistic, that he'd gone to help out an old friend in his adopted country and in part that was true. But there was another reason. A reason he had not acknowledged until this very moment.

He'd been hiding from himself, hiding from intimacy. From sex. From love.

Was he ready to find himself again?

Callie held the key. She had offered her luscious body to him. Unselfishly willing to help him overcome his emotional hang-ups with her sweet cure of light, playful sex.

He wanted what she was offering. He wanted to move forward. He wanted to fully come home. He wanted to belong.

He'd been nursing his wounds for too long. It was time to let all that go. But how could he make love to Callie when he had been hired to guard her? It was his duty to keep her safe and he couldn't keep her safe if his thoughts were constantly on sex.

And your mind isn't on sex right now?

Good point.

"There," he said. "It's done."

Then before she could turn and see exactly how much he wanted her, Luke got out of the tub, splashing water in his wake and made a beeline for the bedroom, closing the bathroom door behind him. He grabbed a change of clothes from the flight bag he'd carried in with him, scooted into the living room and firmly pulled that door closed, as well. He clenched his teeth, more conflicted than he'd been about anything in a very long time.

Desperately, he paced the floor, trying to get control of himself, trying to understand what was happening to him. But when his eyes closed, he saw her again, her beautiful body refracted a hundred times in the mirrored ceiling, the magnetic pull of Callie's image. The longing inside him reined Luke up short. His body shuddered hard.

Inhaling deeply, he recalled the peachy feel of her soft hair beneath his rough fingers, the gut-churning womanly scent of her in his nostrils, the sight of those adorable chocolate-brown eyes narrowing to mere slits in a defiant challenge. He was in over his head with this one, but what a way to drown.

His cock ached. He gulped. This was his fault.

He relived the moments in the bathroom but this time, he acted different. He envisioned himself sliding all the way down into the bathtub with her, soaping her body while he tongued the sweet hollow of her throat. Her imaginary sounds of pleasure echoing softly in his brain.

Her fantasy touch caused his every nerve ending to unravel as he pictured her entwining her arms around his neck, her wet, funky-colored hair plastered to her face. That crooked little mouth tipped up in a sly grin, her head thrown back, exposing her vulnerable neck to the ravages of his mouth.

His imagination escalated the scene.

His erection was pulsating so damned hard he could barely breathe.

Stop this. Stop fantasizing about her.

But he couldn't.

Luke knew that he had to do something or he was going to end up back in the bathtub with her for real. Letting out a long breath, he sank onto the couch.

Thinking of nothing except Callie, he palmed his penis. His rhythm was frantic, desperate, but he had to alleviate the stabbing need that had settled like a stone in his groin from the moment he'd laid eyes on the woman.

This wouldn't take long and then he could have his brain back. Normal, rational, washed free from mind-clogging testosterone.

Clenching his teeth, he shuddered as hot ribbons of milky white ejaculate sprang up, and then spilled down over his fist.

And a single word escaped his lips.

"Callie."

8

A GAME.

That's what Luke needed. A game to learn how to have fun.

Three days and nights had passed since he'd climbed naked into the bathtub and colored her hair. Three days of remembering nothing except that glorious image and three nights of tingling and aching and longing for him as he stonily camped out on her bedroom floor. The numerous book signings blurred into each other. Molly Anne ran her all over L.A. from one event to the next with Luke forever in the background looking out for her.

Tomorrow, they'd be leaving for Santa Barbara, but tonight, she was determined to teach the man how to have fun.

And Callie had the most perfect game in mind. A chase. She would slip away again and see how long it took Luke to follow. Would he realize exactly how much she wanted him to catch her?

And punish her oh, so rightly.

She shivered as goose bumps dotted her arms. She didn't fully understand this compulsion. Why she ached for him so. Why she wanted him. But the need was a hard knot growing inside her at an alarming rate.

She stared at herself in the mirror, still unaccustomed to her new hair color.

Pecan blond.

Her natural hue. How odd that Luke had so uncannily picked out the shade that was almost identical to the one she'd been born with.

She'd just taken a shower after returning from a book signing in Long Beach. Molly Anne had gone back to her own room and Luke was in the sitting area making phone calls. She blew her hair dry, styled it with her fingers then cocked her head to study the effect. The color softened her features and gave her a younger, more feminine look.

She felt calmer somehow. Less wild. She no longer looked like the Midnight Ryder. For a strange moment she felt as if she was staring at both a complete stranger and an old friend.

A very old friend whom she hadn't seen in a very long time. It was the weirdest sensation.

She reached up to redirect the spikes, turning them into soft curls with a flick of the hairbrush. She worked for several minutes and when she was done she could not look away. There was a wistful quality in her eyes that hadn't been there since she was sixteen.

"Who are you?" she whispered.

She stared at the mirror so long, she ended up tripping herself out. She jumped and fled the bathroom, knocking over the vanity chair in her flight to leave.

For no reason, she was panting, out of breath. Lost.

To counterbalance the dramatic change in her appearance and settle her nerves, Callie dug through her suitcase, seeking her most outrageous clothing in an attempt to get back a sense of herself. After dressing in a tight black leather skirt and skimpy striped silk blouse, she then spritzed herself with Sinful, donned lots of silver jewelry and applied an abundance of makeup.

And just to keep it really interesting, she locked the bathroom door from the inside, then returned to the bedroom.

Gingerly picking her way down the ivy-covered trellis in the deepening twilight, she dropped to the garden below. Stepping back and dusting off her palms, she glanced up at the room she'd just vacated.

The bedroom was dark and quiet. The light was on in the adjoining sitting room. She watched a moment, saw Luke's shadow against the window shade when he moved.

Was he coming to check on her?

Her heart churned with crazy excitement. She checked her watch.

Ten past nine.

She waited a few minutes, the ocean breeze brushing softly against her skin, the salty smell filling her nose, stoking her desire. Callie began to tell herself a story.

She was a princess who had been imprisoned by her father, the king, with the best intentions of keeping her safe from marauders. The king had placed a fierce but chaste and loyal knight at her door to protect her while he was away on urgent matters. But the poor princess was bored and sad and lonely. She wanted to have fun. So she disguised herself as a peasant girl and went off to the local tavern to find a lover.

Callie slipped through the darkness, a medieval princess, her breath in her throat, thrilled yet terrified with her new adventure. How long before the knight discovered her gone and came after her?

The handsome, honorable knight.

When he found her, would he roughly drag her back and lock her in her tower once more? Would he listen to her pleas when she begged for her freedom? Would he grant her wish if she offered him the most special reward of her nubile young body?

Callie's stomach muscles tightened. She rounded the corner of the resort hotel and strolled across the cobblestone sidewalk. Was it her imagination or did she hear footfalls behind her?

She paused.

The footsteps stopped.

Luke!

He was coming for her.

She grinned as her pulse rate quickened. Sucking in her breath, hot with anticipation, she hurried off deeper into the night.

"CALLIE?" Luke knocked on the bedroom door. "I'm going to order dinner from room service. What would you like to eat?"

When she didn't answer, he almost didn't knock a second time. He didn't want to awaken her if she had dozed off. But instinct was gnawing at the scruff of his neck. He'd been hired to watch over her and that's what he was going to do.

He placed a hand on the doorknob.

What if she was in there naked, propped up in bed, just waiting for him?

He gulped.

Don't be a coward. You have to check up on her. It's been days now, resisting her should be easier.

Steeling himself, Luke opened the door.

All the lights were out. He blinked, and then after his eyes adjusted to the darkness, his gaze immediately flew to the circular bed.

She wasn't draped there in a femme fatale pose.

He felt both relieved and nervous. She couldn't still be in the bathroom. There was no light under the door. Unless she was in there with candles lit.

"Callie?"

No answer. Not a sound. He'd never known the woman to be so quiet.

Bracing himself for the likely event that she was stark naked in the bathtub doing to herself what he'd been doing to himself the first day here, Luke rapped on the bathroom door with his knuckles.

"Callie? You all right?"

Not a peep.

He jiggled the handle. Locked.

Luke swore under his breath.

What damned game was she playing?

And he knew it was a game. For the woman loved to tease. She wore sensuality like a tight, low-cut sweater. In your face and unapologetic. Even as he admired her ability to embrace her sexuality, he wished she would give it a rest. He was unaccustomed to so much lustiness.

Hesitation had him fisting his hands at his side. "Callie," he called again. "Answer me or I will have to kick the door in."

Which was probably what she was angling for in the first place.

Drama. Action. Excitement.

"Callie!"

His guardian instincts shouldered past his irritation. What if she had slipped in the shower and hit her head?

Luke cocked back his foot, ready to slam his body full force into the doorframe when he caught the movement of something white and fluttery in the darkened recesses of the mirrored ceiling overhead.

The curtains were billowing from the breeze at the open French doors. He was certain that he had closed and locked those doors behind him when he'd checked the suite out earlier upon their return.

Pivoting, he hurried toward the balcony and peered down. The ivy along the trellis was bruised. Someone had just climbed it and there was no question in his mind who that someone was.

Swearing the way only an angry ex-military man could, he tore from the hotel room. He didn't bother with the elevator but plunged down the stairs and tumbled through the emergency exit into the garden.

"Callie," he shouted.

A young couple was taking a stroll on the grounds. They stood and stared at him.

"I'm looking for my fiancé," he said, wearing the lie uncomfortably. "Did you see a woman climb down that trellis?" He waved at the trellis in question. "We, um, had a disagreement."

"Running away from you?" the guy asked.

The woman poked her companion in the ribs with her elbow and shook her head. "No, but there was a man leaving the garden just as we came in."

The blood in Luke's veins turned to ice. Don't panic. A lot of people walk in this garden.

"Where was he at?" Luke asked, trying to act unconcerned.

"Over by that date palm," the guy replied.

Luke thanked the couple and forced himself to saunter casually over to the palm tree they had indicated as if he hadn't a worry in the world.

When he reached the spot, several things became immediately clear. This area had an unrestricted view of Callie's bedroom and there were four cigarette butts crushed out on the ground.

And embedded in the earth damp from ocean spray, was the imprint of a man's shoes.

Someone had been out here for quite some time. Watching.

CALLIE SAT IN A DIM CORNER of Madigan's bar sipping an apple martini and listening to the band on stage.

She was revved up. Anxious.

Already, she'd been approached by three different men looking for companionship and she'd shot them down gently, telling them she was waiting for her fiancé.

One dude made a rude comment about the way she was dressed but the other two took her rejection in stride and moved on.

She glanced at her watch. Almost half an hour had

passed since she'd shimmied down the trellis. What was taking Luke so long?

He was very conscientious about his job. He had to check on her soon. And when he found her gone, he would quickly figure out what she was up to.

The heavy wooden door creaked open and the stalwart knight stalked over the threshold. Sir Galahad.

Clearly, he was a warrior on the hunt for dragons to slay. From her position at a corner table she could see him, but he could not yet see her.

Her gaze traveled over his tall, imposing frame, took in his broad shoulders, the commanding expression on his ruggedly masculine face. He was a man you dared not toy with.

And yet, she had dared. Setting this illicit game in motion.

Would he pick up the gauntlet? Would he play?

His features were Nordic, but his coloring was not. High cheekbones, proud nose, black hair, even blacker eyes. He was an odd combination of light and dark. North and south. He was a paradox. World-weary, yet inexperienced all at the same time.

He made her pulse strum with the most frantic rhythm.

But what most commanded her attention, besides his strong presence, was his mouth. Sensuously full lips.

Infinitely kissable.

He wore his warrior costume. Black T-shirt, green camouflage pants, combat boots. His biceps were so big they strained against the seams of his T-shirt.

Ah. Here he was then. *Her* knight.

When had she started thinking of him so possessively?

He moved into the bar, turning his head from side to side, searching for her. She felt a little thrill of fear. Not from him, but from her rampant fantasies. She tensed, clenching the edge of the table with her fingers, waiting for him to spot her.

His black-eyed gaze met hers.

Callie was totally unprepared for her body's explosive reaction. He raked his eyes over her, making her feel as if she was not wearing a single stitch of clothing. She trembled as violently as if he had just cupped her bare breasts in the palms of his rough hands.

He came toward her.

All the other sounds in the bar disappeared. She heard only his boots treading across the wooden floor.

The heavy noise matched the rhythm of the blood pushing through her veins, thick with lust.

His eyes were ablaze with anger and yet at the same time, he looked relieved to find her. That was when she realized the anger had actually been fear. He'd thought the stalker had gotten her.

She felt contrite for worrying him but not contrite enough to back off the game. She held his gaze and they were joined as surely as if he had just slid his hard angular body into her soft round one.

The princess and the knight.

A sweet fantasy come alive.

Several people moved between them, heading for the dance floor but Luke was taller than all of them. His head towered high above the throng and he never once lost eye contact with her.

Callie sucked in a breath as she imagined his eager hands slipping up under her skirt, caressing her hot bare thighs. Did he have any idea what wickedness was on her mind?

The knight was upon her now. Dragging out the chair opposite from her, he sat down without being invited. That was the way of the warrior. Warriors took what they wanted.

Did he want her the way she wanted him?

He said nothing.

Neither did she.

The band played on.

They continued to stare into each other's eyes. Callie's daydreams ran wild as she imagined his hand not stopping at her thigh, but creeping higher in the darkness, eventually finding its way to the warm soft cleft between her legs.

She squirmed.

Her nipples hardened against the fantasy. She wasn't wearing a bra and the nubs strained against the luxurious silk of her low-neck blouse.

She imagined his masculine mouth covering hers the way it had in the airport. His tongue dueling with hers until she was left too breathless to even beg him for sweet release.

Callie made a whimpering sound at the back of her throat and shook her head to rid it of her reverie. But it would not go. The vision clung to her brain, sticky as a spider's web.

In reality, Luke simply sat there with his arms crossed over his chest, watching her, waiting for a response.

But in her mind…he was kissing her the way she'd always longed to be kissed.

He took her lip between his teeth and nipped it lightly. Punishing her playfully for running away from him a second time since she'd known him. He dragged his mouth down over her chin, kissing the column of her neck until he reached the fluttering pulse at the hollow of her throat, and then slowly flicking his tongue back and forth.

Lower he went. Lower, and then lower still. Back and forth. Tongue licking, tasting, teasing.

She pretended that right there in the bar, he was ripping open her blouse with his teeth, buttons popping everywhere.

"What'll you have to drink?" From out of nowhere a waitress appeared at Luke's side, order pad in hand.

"Nothing, thank you," he replied without glancing at her. "We were just leaving."

"He'll have a beer." Callie smiled sweetly at the server. "And I'll have another apple martini."

"I don't want a beer."

"You need to relax."

"I'm on the job."

"One beer isn't going to hurt you."

The waitress looked from Luke to Callie and back again. "Which is it?"

"I'm not leaving until you have a drink," Callie told Luke.

"You will if I sling you over my shoulder and carry you out of here."

"Hmm, you might be right." Callie tapped her index finger against her chin. "That does sound like fun. My breasts smashed flat against your strong, broad back. Your big palm splayed across my fanny holding me in place while I kick and scream for help."

"You wouldn't dare."

"Try me. I live for dares."

The room was dark but she knew he was blushing, and probably sweating, too.

"I'll have that beer," Luke told the waitress. "Whatever's on tap."

The waitress nodded and left.

"See." Callie beamed at him. "Was that so hard?"

"Why do you always have to say the most shocking thing that pops into your brain?"

"It's how I make my living."

He shook his head. "Strange way for a woman to make a living."

"Oh, like it's okay for male shock jocks to get down and dirty but not a woman?"

"That's not what I meant."

"What did you mean?"

"You're above that sort of juvenile stuff, Callie. You're smart and attractive and you've got a lot going for you. You could be anything you wanted to be."

"This is what I want to be," she stubbornly insisted, even as his compliment lit up her heart. At the same time she wondered if she really did want to spend the rest of her life trying to shock people. Even with her show toned down and retooled for the morning spot at KSXX, she'd still be expected to say the outrageous.

"I guess if you tell yourself something long enough it's bound to become your reality."

"Oh, like you're one to talk. Mr. I-can't-have-sex-if-I'm-not-madly-in-love. Watch out, you could get a nose-bleed up there on your high horse."

He pressed his lips together. She watched the play of emotions cross his face, saw him bite back his anger. "I really do like your hair," he said. "It's gentle."

"Gentle is not my shtick."

"Maybe it should be."

"Don't hold your breath waiting for that to happen." What did he mean maybe she should be more gentle? She was plenty gentle. Just ask…hmm, she couldn't think of anyone who would confirm her gentleness. Not even her mom.

Damn him. Luke had the disturbing knack of getting straight to the heart of things. Things you didn't partic-ularly want anybody getting straight to the heart of.

"I can be gentle," she finally said.

"I didn't say you couldn't," he said mildly.

Okay, so she wasn't particularly gentle. It wasn't as if she had small kids or pets or anything. No one missed her gentleness.

Shake him up. Find a way to get even. Make him stop looking at you as if you've disappointed him in some major way.

Still holding his sharp-edged gaze, Callie kicked off her shoe, raised her leg and planted her right foot firmly against his crotch. Luckily the tablecloth was long enough to hide what she was doing from the other pat-rons. Then again, she liked to shock people. If anyone saw her, big hairy deal. What's the worst that could happen? They would get thrown out of the place. Oh, boo-hoo.

Luke grimaced and his pupils narrowed, but that was the only reaction allowed to cross his face. The blush had disappeared.

She traced the fly of his zipper with her bare toes. She got to him that time. He inhaled on a rough whistle of air.

He was looking straight into her and she was staring right back. He didn't move. His hands were clenched on top of the table. He was obviously waiting.

But not protesting.

Was he too stunned? Or did he like what she was doing to him too much to complain?

Callie managed to hook her big toe over the top of his zipper and slowly began to inch it down.

She felt him swell.

And she couldn't keep from smiling. Her ability to control him with her feminine power was exceptionally rewarding.

"Goodness," she whispered. "Exactly how big does it get?"

His expression never changed but his thigh muscle tensed beneath the sole of her foot. His stare was beginning to unnerve her.

He leaned in closer until his forehead almost touched hers and said in a low, sultry voice. "How big can you handle?"

Callie jumped. Okay. So that's how it was going to be. Someone better turn up the air-conditioning fast because she was starting to puddle.

She edged his zipper down far enough to slip her toes inside his fly. When she felt velvety skin and rock-hard flesh, she realized at once he was not wearing underwear.

Her eyes widened. "You're freeballing?"

"Excuse me?"

Either she was imagining things or a thin line of perspiration was riding Luke's upper lip. The man was just as turned on as she was.

Good. She was glad she wasn't alone in this exquisite torture.

"No underwear," she said. "Freeballing."

"Oh. No. No underwear."

"I would never have thought it of you, Mr. Cardasian. Considering what a stickler you are for protocol."

"I got accustomed to…er…freeballing as you put it, in Limbasa. Cotton shortage. I learned to like the freedom."

This new knowledge unnerved her. She'd thought she had him pegged right down to white cotton boxer briefs. Boy, was she wrong. What else did she not know about him?

"Ah," she said, keeping things light. "So you are trainable. I was beginning to have my doubts."

And with that, she curled her toes into his zipper.

He hissed through clenched teeth. "I hope you realize that, thanks to you, we're stuck here for a while."

Both his hands were still fisted on the tabletop and damned if his arms weren't trembling from the effort of keeping them in place.

The look in his eyes changed and along with it the intensity of the tugging sensation in her belly. There was a flicker of something golden in his eyes, something wild and unexpected.

The form of his lips changed, his posture, the slant of his eyebrows.

He was someone else entirely. Sir Galahad no more. This man was darker. Had seen things no one had any business seeing.

She swallowed audibly, her foot still cocked on his very masculine trigger. What now? Where did she go from here?

Slowly, she began to draw her foot away, inching her toes out of his zipper.

But before she knew what he was doing, Luke shoved his hand under the table and grabbed hold of her ankle as if he had the wrist of a kid caught rummaging in the cookie jar.

"Not so fast."

Her eyes widened. "Y…yes?" For once she felt less than confident.

She'd started this game but she had no idea what the rules were. She expected to keep pushing him, backing him into a corner. She hadn't expected him to be aggressive.

He's not a fantasy, he's a real man. And I think the Midnight Ryder just swam into deep water.

She hadn't thought it possible, but she'd shocked herself.

"You got us stirred up. Now what do you intend to do to alleviate the situation?" His brows dipped down in a V.

Was he suggesting what she thought he was suggesting? A hand job under the table? Or was he expecting something even more daring?

She licked her lips.

He nodded, confirming her suspicions.

She had a quick mental flash of sliding out of her chair and onto her knees. Ducking below the table, she'd give him the most fabulous blow job of his life right here in the bar.

She could have sworn her heart stopped. She couldn't feel it beating.

"Well?" Luke asked.

Callie couldn't imagine what might have happened next if the waitress hadn't reappeared, smacking the thick mug of beer down onto the table saying, "Here's your Michelob, sir."

9

DETERMINED TO WIN this battle of wills, Luke had called Callie's bluff and given her a dose of her own medicine, even though it had been difficult for him to make such a brazen suggestion.

And he could have sworn that, for a moment, even though she had swiftly hidden her surprise, he had shocked the famous lady shock jock. Of course if she had gone on her knees and slipped under the table to give him the blow job he had hinted at, he would not have allowed her to go through with it.

He wasn't that kind of guy.

"Too bad about the interruption," she murmured. "For a little while there I thought we were getting somewhere with your sex education."

"Finish your drink and let's get out of here," he said. "Before something happens that neither one of us can handle."

"Oooh." Her eyes sparkled mischievously. "Is that a threat or a promise?"

She lightly feathered her toes over his zipper, stroking him through his pants. He was harder than he had ever been in his life.

Man, but she was something else. The more he learned about her, the more he wanted to know. And the more he knew about her, the more possessive he felt toward her.

This new realization needled him. Damn, but he was horny for her. And that couldn't be good.

He would like to blame his weakness on the lack of sex, but Luke knew his vulnerability where Callie was concerned ran far deeper than that. Before meeting her, he had never had a problem with self-control or with keeping his mind on his job. Now all he could think about was making love to her.

He studied her in the lighting cast from the television set nearby. Whenever the image on the screen would change, so would the color of the light falling against her cheek.

Her face was a canvas of shifting hues. First green, then blue, pink and then a blue-green combo flickered over her freckles, her delicate bones, the lithe musculature, and the faint blue traces of a vein running beneath the petal softness of her jaw.

"What is it?" she asked.

"What?"

"You're looking at me weird."

"The television." Luke gestured. "It's bathing your face."

They both turned in their chairs to glance at the mounted television set on the wall. A group of rowdy guys were clustered around the bar, popping peanuts and hooting appreciatively as the image of glamorous Brooke Burnett filled the screen.

"Brooke Burnett here," the reporter said. "With the

latest dish on red-hot sex guru, Callie Ryder. I'm sorry guys, but for all of you who've been drooling over this luscious babe, I have bad news. Earlier this week I caught up with Ms. Ryder and discovered she just got engaged to sexy New York City bodyguard, Luke Cardasian."

The television screen flickered and then there he and Callie were, kissing at the airport as if it was the end of the world and their last chance for sex.

In the segment, Luke looked totally addled by lust. His eyes were heavy with it and he was consuming Callie's mouth as if he'd been lost in the desert for six months with nothing to eat.

His ears burned with shame. What had he been thinking? Clearly, he hadn't been thinking at all.

Brooke Burnett was still talking but Luke was barely listening. He was too busy kicking himself. "The Midnight Ryder might have surprised her listeners by getting engaged so quickly," Brooke said. "But she's about to get one very big surprise of her own."

Callie sat up straight, finally dropping her foot to the floor, her eyes fixed on the television. "Surprise? What surprise?"

The surprise for Luke was how disappointed he felt now that her foot was gone and he was left with a rock-hard erection and nothing to do about it.

"Ms. Ryder's co-worker, and the current reigning king of talk radio, Buck Bryson, got the boot two days ago," Brooke's smile widened. "His ratings had been slipping as the Midnight Ryder's have soared. A little bird told me that America's number-one radio time slot belongs to you if you want it, Callie."

"Buck got fired?" Callie blinked.

"Sounds like you're in line for a promotion."

"I didn't expect this."

"Do you want the promotion?"

"It's what I've been working for all my life," she said, but she did not look like someone whose life's dream was on the verge of being realized.

"Yeah, but do you want it?"

Callie glanced at him and in her eyes Luke did not see pleasure or happiness but rather doubt and confusion. He didn't believe she wanted the job.

"I gotta go find Molly Anne." She sprang up from the table.

Luke started to get up but banged his knee against the top of the table and the pain forced him back down in his seat. "Dammit to hell."

Callie was already halfway across the room.

"Wait," he called and pushed himself up from the table again, but realized his fly was still unzipped at the same time his cell phone rang.

He snatched the phone off his belt with one hand while tugging up his zipper with the other. "Cardasian," he barked into the receiver.

"It's Zack."

"Yeah? What is it? I'm kinda busy at the moment."

"No doubt. Just when were you going to tell me that you were engaged to Callie Ryder?"

CALLIE HAD NO IDEA why she felt so panicked. The news about Buck Bryson getting fired should have brought rejoicing. Instead, she felt claustrophobic, as if the walls of that darkened nightclub were closing in on her.

Barb had even predicted it, but she'd been sure her engineer was only dreaming. In its current format *Let's Talk About Sex* wasn't suited for morning drive-to-work talk radio and that's why she'd never really worried about being given Buck's slot. Had Barb been privy to secret information? Had she known something even then? Or was she just that intuitive?

Callie had to get out. Had to get to Molly Anne and find out if she was going to be offered Buck's job for real.

Because she didn't want it.

She heard Luke shout for her to stop but her mind couldn't even process it. She was freaked.

If she let herself get swept away by Molly Anne and the radio station, not to mention the media hype, then she would lose herself forever. She would be a trash-talking shock jock for the rest of her life.

She'd been born with a lively, energetic nature. As a child, she'd valued happiness above success, but after her parents' divorce, her teenage rebellion and her own failures at finding love, she'd learned to value status and be more concerned with her reputation and with showing off than anything more substantial.

And for a while it had worked, but suddenly she felt as if she'd taken a wrong turn at some crucial juncture and if she kept cruising down this road she would never find her true essence.

She'd used her job, her persona as a way to avoid pain. She stayed on the move, ever in pursuit of new and exciting experiences. This characteristic had helped her enjoy the moment while evading emotional depth. She'd used her enthusiasm and her confidence as a shield for the vulnerability lurking beneath the surface.

While this defense mechanism had protected her, it had also kept her contained. Until lately, she hadn't even given much consideration to the difference between a want and a need. Instinct told her she would not be okay if her needs were not met. But did she need to be a shock jock? Or was it a desire she'd convinced herself of a long time ago and now she'd outgrown it? She was on the verge of real stardom and yet deep inside she still felt unsatisfied and frustrated.

Why?

Her heels made sharp click-click-click noises as she ran for the door. Her chest felt as if it had a band around it, cinching tighter with each passing moment. By the time she plunged through the door and out onto the street she could scarcely breathe.

"Callie!" Luke called.

She shook her head. She needed to be alone. She had to think. Why was she overreacting?

"Callie, stop!" Luke commanded.

But she did not. She ran headlong into the street, her heart slapping lickety-split.

And then she heard it, the sound of a car engine being gunned.

Startled, she froze as headlights barreled toward her.

LUKE DIVED AND PUSHED Callie out of the way of the speeding sedan, shoving her to safety.

He lay atop her where they had landed on the grassy

median. He quickly turned his head, saw the sedan careen around the corner, tires screeching, too fast to catch a glimmer of the license plate number.

Luke rolled off Callie, got to his feet and helped her up. Holding one arm around her waist, he dusted off the back of her clothes. He was shaking inside, terrified for her safety.

"Are you all right?" he asked. "Are you hurt?"

"The grass cushioned the blow. I think I'm okay."

"You sure?" His eyes met hers.

"I'm fine. Just dandy." And then she burst into tears. "Damned drunkard."

"I don't think it was a drunk," Luke said. He was concerned for her, but angry with himself. He shouldn't have taken the time to answer his cell phone. If he'd just been one more step behind her, Callie wouldn't be here.

"You think it's the guy who's been sending the threats?"

He nodded and reached for his cell phone. "I'm calling the police." After he made the call, he turned to find her shivering in the cool ocean breeze. A pale half-moon shone down, covering her in a soft glow.

She looked at him, her eyes wide and scared. "Hold me."

He was startled to see her looking defenseless. He pulled her to his chest, wrapped her in his arms. She was trembling so much he hadn't the heart to chastise her for running out of the bar without him. Clearly, she'd learned an important lesson.

She clung to his waist and the scent of her filled his nose. Gone was the tough, trash-talking woman who liked to stun and in her place was a soft vulnerable Callie.

His gut wrenched and he loosened his grip.

"Don't let go," she whimpered into the hollow of his neck.

And that was the moment Luke figured out that her sassy, bad-girl bravado was actually protecting a very tender heart. The plaintive look in her eyes made him realize just how much he wanted to protect her.

"I won't," he promised. "I'm not going anywhere."

For several minutes they simply stood there in the moonlight, waiting for the police to show up to take their statements, gazing into each other's faces. It was the oddest sensation, but he felt knocked off balance. Drunk even. Impossible. He'd only had three swallows of his Michelob. But how else could he explain this feeling?

What was it about her that made it seem as if his throat was suddenly full of his heart? He hovered in terrible limbo, knowing he shouldn't kiss her, but certain he was going to.

He captured her sweet face between his palms and was thinking about capturing her mouth with his own when the patrol car pulled into Madigan's parking lot. He was both disappointed and relieved at the interruption.

A uniformed officer got out of the squad car. "You the guy who called about the drunk driver?"

"Yes."

The officer took their statements, but since Luke wasn't able to give him the license plate number, the policeman didn't hold out much hope they'd catch the guy. Luke told him about the threats Callie had been receiving. The officer seemed inclined to believe it was nothing more than a drunk driver, but he instructed Luke to call the department immediately if anything suspicious occurred. Fifteen minutes after he'd arrived, the officer departed.

Luke turned to face Callie, which was his first mistake, and his second one was believing he could maintain any objectivity where she was concerned. She stared at him with such knowledge he felt as if she were peering right inside his soul. As if she'd gained unauthorized access to his deepest secrets.

"Take me back to the hotel," Callie begged and ran her hot pink tongue over his lips, pressing her lithe form against his solid one. "I need you tonight."

At that moment, he knew he was going to take her to bed.

It was wrong. No question about that. But he'd spent the last three nights fighting off his desires and the last twenty-nine years doing the right thing, staying on the right track so he seemed almost destined for this one slipup, this single mistake.

He would probably regret it later. He was fully aware of the potential consequences, but he could not stop himself. She needed the comfort of his body and he was desperate to comfort her.

Without another word, Luke scooped her into his arms and walked back to their hotel. She entwined her fingers around his neck, hanging on as if he was the only thing standing between her and nothingness.

He had to admit he liked the feeling of taking care of her. Protecting her. Being her hero. But would he know what to do with her once he had her in bed? He didn't want to fumble, didn't want to make a blunder. He wanted everything to be perfect.

She knew her way around a sex act and he did not. What if he embarrassed himself? Worse, what if he disappointed her? Hellacious thing for a man. To be almost thirty and little more than a virgin.

Don't think about your deficiencies. What is the one thing you can give her that no one else can?

That was an easy one. He could fulfill her fantasies. Give her everything she wanted. He would be like the stable man in the illicit stories she told. He would use his fingers to trace a road map over her body. Lingering where she wanted him to linger. Skimming where she begged him to skim. Learning exactly how to trip her trigger.

Luke hurried, Callie snug in his arms. They barely got into the suite and she was tearing at his clothes.

He claimed possession of her mouth, owning it, staking it.

Her lips were velvety soft and so damned feminine. Her teeth parted, letting him in. He kissed her passionately, fiercely.

Too fast, too fast. He knew he was plunging ahead quickly but he did not know how to slow down. His body was filled with the pressure that had been building moment by moment.

Her spontaneity was attractive. She was an epicurean of life and she was everything he was not. She was open, expressive, unrestrained. She enlivened everyone around her. Some might consider her a flake but Luke thought of her as dynamic and free. He wished he could be so flexible, so full of life. She was real and true with her sexuality and he admired her for it.

Callie slid to her knees before him, a wild glow of excitement in her eyes. The contour of her lips changed, her posture was looser. Her fingers worked frantically, undoing his pants. She tugged his trousers to his knees and he kicked out of them.

His cock was rock hard.

He flinched at the first touch of her mouth, but her lips felt so hot and wet around his shaft that Luke couldn't help groaning. The sensation was achingly sweet and so powerful he had to lace his fingers through her hair to keep from toppling over.

He was a lucky, lucky bastard. No doubt about it. He looked down at her and his heart stuttered.

He swayed.

She spread her hands over his buttocks to help steady him, her fingers splaying into his flesh. And when her mouth latched on to him with force, Luke's eyes rolled back in his head. She was lapping and suckling as if she could never get enough of him. He knew he couldn't get enough of her.

She tickled the small of his back with one hand, cupped his balls with the other. Luke almost yelped. It felt that damned incredible.

Systemically, she set about dismantling him with her mouth.

He felt embarrassed then and in spite of his body's intense ache, he wanted to reach down to pull her to her feet but he was ensnared in a chaotic whirlwind of sensation. He was afraid and he was afraid to admit he was afraid. He wanted his serenity back. He wanted to feel balanced again. This powerful sexual attraction caused him an inner dishevelment that went against his honorable intentions.

Luke moaned as the heat escalated inside him. Her rhythm picked up. Her hands slid all over his body. Indescribable, this intimacy. His chest expanded, tightened. It was unlike anything he'd ever experienced. This took the meaning of sex to a whole new level for him.

"Yes," he hissed as she moved back and forth, her hair a soft glide beneath his fingers. "Yes, yes, yes."

Callie worked her magic with her fingers, her tongue leading him into uncharted territory. He was on sensory overload as she gently guided him to a paradise he'd only dreamed of.

But this wasn't a dream. The warm wetness of her mouth, the sweet taste of her kiss still lingering on his tongue, her heavenly feminine scent, the sound of the ocean wafting in through the open French doors. This new awareness of him, of her was breaking up his brittle outer shell. All the old failures and disappointments fell away.

She was beyond beauty to him. She was pure life, pure joy. She and her sensual impulses merged together against all the rules of proper conduct. Her mouth moved over him without caution or fear. She pushed him past his knowledge of himself. He had never before been so physically possessed. Her movements shook his world. The walls of the hotel room seemed to ripple. Could this be an earthquake?

No. The ground did not tremble, only his body.

Luke was nervous and exalted and awed. He accepted the inevitable.

"Yes," she murmured, "That's right. Release all your preconceived notions."

How had she discerned the mental shift in him? His acceptance. The letting go?

In the distance, Luke heard the soft hum of honeybees singing, calling him to their hive. He shook his head but the humming intensified, growing louder and stronger the more Callie plied her tongue against him.

Luke frowned. What was that noise?

A vibrator? Whoa. Where had she gotten a vibrator?

He stiffened, suddenly nervous about what was going on down there. This was all new territory for him and he wasn't quite sure he trusted her completely.

"Callie?"

"Shh," she whispered against his shaft. "Shh."

He stiffened and almost told her to stop but then he swallowed hard, took a leap of faith and decided to trust her.

The humming drew closer, a small round cylinder buzzing over his buttocks, his balls and the area in between until he could no longer tell vibration from fingers or tongue. His knees were quaking and he was as loaded and hot as he could ever be.

Past thinking, with no coherent thought residing in his head, he was nothing but cock and ass and balls.

Vibrating. Humming. Buzzing with sensation.

Relentlessly, Callie pushed him forward. He was aching, gushing, throbbing, beating. He threw back his head and let loose with a primal cry, pleading for release from this magnificent torture, for the ecstasy he could almost touch.

Tingling. Pounding. Rushing.

Soon. Please, please let it be soon. It had better be or he was going to drop dead from need.

And then, just like that, it was upon him.

Luke tumbled. Jerking and trembling into the abyss, hurtling across time and space. Lost. Enveloped by the chasm. The earth, the sky, the air, the ocean exploded in a ball of white-hot rapture.

He peered down, blinked. He could barely see. Callie was sitting at his feet, smiling coyly, her lips glistening creamy and wet. She winked at him and swallowed his essence like a greedy cat at the milk.

Luke pitched forward onto his knees and then collapsed onto his side. He lay there sweating, shuddering, panting for breath.

The honeybees were gone. His cock emptied. He tucked himself into a fetal position while he tried to wrap his mind around what had just happened.

Callie curled up on the carpet beside him. She spooned against his back. For a long while they just lay there together, not speaking, waiting for him to recover.

When at last he could rouse himself, Luke lifted his head, gave her a satisfied grin and said, "Now, it's your turn."

10

"LET'S TAKE A BATH," Luke suggested. "I've been fantasizing about getting you in one ever since you invited me to join you there."

Callie nodded, still too overwhelmed by what she'd just done to him to even speak. She glanced up to find Luke's eyes on hers, scanning her inch by inch. It was clear that he did not think any less of her. In fact, he looked quite pleased.

He took her by the hand and led her into the bathroom. She meekly acquiesced. He seated her at the vanity, turning the chair around so she could watch him. She was supposed to be teaching him, but it seemed he was the one giving the lessons.

His bare taut buttocks flexed as he moved. The pale skin on his bare butt contrasted to the tan above his waist. She went breathless staring at his abs. The man had to spend hours a day at the gym. Mesmerized, Callie could not look away. He put any male model she had ever seen to shame.

He was glorious. All biceps and triceps and glutes and hamstrings. Take that, Adonis. She couldn't ever remember having such a well-built lover. She would remember this body for a long time to come.

And his face!

Straight out of a fantasy. His jaw was square, his cheekbones prominent. His dark hair glistened in the light, the severe short cut suited him. There was nothing frivolous about him.

Luke drew the bath, adding the foaming bath beads he found on the counter. They scented the air with the smell of fruit and sunshine.

"Music," he said. "We need music."

Callie pointed out that there was a stereo system in the sitting area with surround-sound speakers that were piped into the bathroom. First-class honeymoon suite in a five-star resort. Not too shabby.

"Be right back," he said and disappeared.

The bathtub was heart shaped and decadently big. You could host a small orgy in the thing if you had a mind to do such a thing. Callie sat in the chair, watching the tub fill up, smelling the scent of peaches and strawberries and thinking about Luke.

Soon, the soft sounds of classical music trickled through the wall and Luke was back with two glasses of champagne, one clasped in each hand. He set the flutes down, and then lit the trio of white coconut-scented candles on the wall mount over the tub.

"Where'd you get champagne?"

"Minibar."

She arched an eyebrow. "That doesn't sound like you at all."

"I know, I know. Too expensive, but this is a special occasion. The first time we make love."

His smile was so tender, so genuine, something inside Callie pricked uncomfortably.

"Luke," she said. "We have to talk."

"Uh-oh. That doesn't sound good."

"Sit." She waved at the edge of the tub.

So he sat.

"Listen." Callie paused, not knowing quite how to say what she had to say.

"Got both ears trained on you, sweetheart."

"I think we should get something straight before we take this any further."

"What's on your mind?"

How many times had she given this I'm-not-the-marrying-kind-so-don't-go-falling-in-love-with-me speech? It was never easy, but this time, it was particularly difficult. She liked Luke. More than she had any right to like him but this had to be said. She didn't want to set him up for unrealistic expectations.

"I just wanted to make sure you understand, this thing between us." She motioned from her to him and back again. "Is temporary. A good time. Nothing more."

"I understand."

"Do you? Because I don't want you getting a broken heart."

"I'm not going to get a broken heart." He scowled. "I know what I'm doing."

"You might. If we go down this road we're going to have a lot of intimate fun and I'm worried you'll confuse a good time with something more than it is."

"I'm inexperienced, not an idiot."

"Considering your ideas about sex and love and all

that…" She was trying not to notice that he was growing rock hard again. "And you're pretending to be my fiancé. It could set you up for a fall—big-time."

"Beliefs can change."

"So you promise not to fall in love with me?" She caught her breath, studied his face. "I won't do this thing if you don't promise."

"We shouldn't be doing this thing anyway," he said. "From a logical point of view."

"Screw logic. Just promise me."

"I promise. There's only one thing I want from you, Callie Ryder."

"And what is that, Luke Cardasian?" she whispered, leaning forward.

"To learn everything I can about sex."

"All right, then." She straightened. "As long as we're on the same page."

"Let's toast." He raised his champagne glass. "To Callie Ryder's world-class sex lessons."

She forced a smile, clinked her glass against his and took a sip of champagne.

"To world-class sex," she echoed and wondered why she felt so empty inside.

He drained his champagne in one long swallow and rested the glass on the bathroom counter. "I'm ready for lesson 101."

"Hold on to your horses, mister."

"You and the stable analogies."

"It's a girl thing," she said and stuck out her tongue.

Then she got to her feet and slowly began to take off her clothes. She had performed lots of stripteases before and she'd never been self-conscious. Not even the first time she'd tried it.

But now, she found herself hesitating, fumbling at her buttons, feeling unsure of herself. What was wrong? Was it because Luke was looking at her as if he needed a pen and paper to take notes?

She rushed through the process, anxious to get it over with. He didn't seem to notice that he had received the abbreviated version of her burlesque moves.

Even the look of frank appreciation in his eyes when he saw her naked did nothing to allay her uneasiness. Turning her back to him, she slipped under the water, grateful to hide her body beneath the bubbles.

"Can I get in there with you?" he asked, after she had sunk down, closed her eyes and letting the effects of the heat and champagne relax her.

Slowly, she opened one eye. He was standing beside the tub, smiling tenderly.

See there. That smile. That smile was why she didn't believe him when he promised that he wasn't going to fall in love with her. His smile was too trusting and too hungry by half.

She almost told him to go away and leave her alone. Before she could say no, he was already dipping a foot into the water.

What was she doing in the bathtub with a man she'd known for only seventy-two hours? Normally she wasn't hung up about sex or time limits or dating rules. But she had never gone to bed with someone after having only known them for a few days.

It felt weirdly wicked and forbiddenly fantastic and totally taboo.

Luke sank to his knees in the tub. He leaned forward, his chest above hers. He pressed his lips flush against her ear. His beard stubble tickled her skin.

"Teach me," he whispered. "Show me how you like it. I'm here to please and this is all about you. Tell me everything about your body."

Callie shuddered. This big man, kneeling in front of her, willingly admitting his inexperience, turning to her for guidance, wanting nothing more than to pleasure her.

"Bathe me," she said. "Wash me clean."

Now why had she said that?

But what was it that she wanted him to wash away? Her past? The possibility of a future with him? Or maybe she wished he would scrub off the Midnight Ryder. Expose the real Callie beneath the facade.

That notion left her feeling much more vulnerable than her nakedness ever could.

She nearly stopped the game right then and there. Almost sloshed from the water, grabbed the white terrycloth bathrobe from the hook beside the tub and dashed out the door.

Almost.

Something in his eyes held her in place. Something she could not quite identify. Hadn't she learned anything yet? Whenever she ran from him she got into trouble. Better to stay here and see this thing through.

Luke leaned back against the tub, bent his knees up and planted his feet on either side of her hips. Her legs were extended underneath his. The heart-shaped tub was plenty big enough, and her limbs short enough, for her to stretch out completely.

Her breasts floated on the water. Not too small, not too big. Perky and peeking through the bubbles.

Luke was eyeing them surreptitiously, trying not to be obvious, but the heat of his gaze caused her nipples to pucker and extend.

The scented white candles on the counter flickered, the smell of coconut in the air. The music was fluid, sweet. Vivaldi, she guessed, not up on her classical composers.

Or perhaps Pachelbel. Soft and low.

High-tech. High-class. Little Callie Ryder from Winslow, Georgia had never even dreamed of such luxury. Candles and music and champagne and a heart-shaped tub. It smacked of romance.

It smacked of love.

She had to do something to shake this romantic feeling. What they needed was serious sex. Now.

"Soap me up," she said.

He fumbled for the soap, lost it, caught it and then rubbed it against the washcloth he plucked from the towel rack beside them.

Two apple martinis and a glass of champagne on an empty stomach, a near sideswipe from a careening car, mixed with the sleepy effects of the steaming bath and the blow job she'd given him, conspired to make her woozy and drunk with the moment.

She was alive and in the bath with the most incredibly tender tough guy ever to walk into her corner of the world. Even her most avid listeners wouldn't have bought into this fantasy. It was too unbelievable.

"Close your eyes," he whispered, "and tilt your head back."

When she obeyed, he moved above her, simultaneously kissing her eyelids with his hot mouth while his rough masculine hands stroked the washcloth gently along her throat.

He cleaned her arms and shoulders and fingers, brushing and caressing and massaging her skin with the cloth. Then he bathed her feet and her ankles, slid slowly up her calves to her knees and on to her sensitive, throbbing thighs. Callie bit down on her bottom lip as he lingered too long on her inner thighs.

She kept her eyes closed, savoring the sensation. She was good at this, enjoying sensual pleasure. Always had been. She saw nothing wrong with pleasing her body, had no hang-ups, guilt or inhibitions associated with physical release.

Where Callie got tangled up was when the guy wanted more. A commitment. A promise. Happily-ever-after. She really didn't believe in any of that. Her parents' sorry marriage had been proof enough that lust makes promises that love can never keep.

So she never made promises about love and things had rocked on just fine. This was the way she liked it.

Just as she liked what was going on below her neck. Luke was doing such a bang-up job of swirling that warm washcloth over her belly.

Was he headed up or down?

Her body tensed and then started tingling as she tried to anticipate his next move.

He surprised her by abandoning the washcloth on her

belly and reaching to skim his fingers over her face, outlining her bones with the pads of his fingertips. A blind man learning Braille.

Then he cupped her face in both his hands and he stopped moving. She wanted to open her eyes, to see what was happening, but she was too afraid to meet his gaze. Too scared of the expression she might spot in his eyes.

She could feel his breath on her cheeks. He said nothing. Neither did she.

A minute ticked by. Pachelbel or Vivaldi shifted into Mozart. Him, she recognized. She'd had an instructor in college who insisted on playing Mozart while they took exams.

Finally, she could stand the suspense no longer and cautiously pried open one eye.

Luke's face was right in front of hers and he was looking at her as if she was one of the seven wonders of the world.

Stop looking at me like that, she wanted to shout but didn't. I'm not unique or special or great.

He kissed her and cupped her breasts in his warm, soapy palms. Her nipples beaded even harder beneath his hands and he thumbed them ever so slightly.

They exhaled at the same time, breathing out each other's air.

She thought he was quivering, then realized it was her, shaking so hard the water rippled.

"What now?" he whispered. "What do you want me to do next?"

Tell him to get out of the tub, to dry off, to go sleep on the sofa.

But she didn't do that. She wanted him as badly as he wanted her.

Just don't let it mean anything. Make him understand that.

"Luke," she murmured.

"Yes?"

"This really is just about sex you know."

"I know."

"I don't want you to read any more into this than there is."

"Don't worry. You've made that abundantly clear. So just tell me what to do next. Your every wish is my command."

Her mouth was so dry she could barely answer. She wet her lips. "Touch me."

"Where?"

"Down there." She parted her thighs.

He slipped his hand between them, his fingers curling around her mound. He watched her expectantly, awaiting more instructions.

"Put your middle finger inside me."

He dipped his middle finger over her budding cleft but did not plunge past into her warm moistness.

"In me," she whispered.

Instead he put the slightest of pressure against her clit. *Go in, go in.*

He did not. He just sat there, staring into her eyes, finger cocked and ready to make her beg. Ah, how quickly he was catching on.

She sucked air.

Then, with the joint of his middle finger riding her

most sensitive button, he slid the rest of the finger inside her.

She pushed her pelvis against his hand, slid down in the tub until the water was lapping at her ears. She was on the edge of a dark peak, surrounded by the feel of his finger, the warm wetness of the water, the smell of coconut, the sound of Mozart and the sight of his gorgeous, muscular body. It had been a long time since she'd felt so engulfed.

Callie wanted him too much. The passion was consuming her. She'd slipped too far. Water filled her nose.

Sputtering, she sat up, sneezing water and wiping the soap bubbles from her eyes, killing the moment.

"I'm sorry," she apologized.

For nothing, for everything. For causing his downfall. For corrupting a principled man.

"Nothing to be sorry about."

"Yes there is, I should never have…"

"Shh," he murmured, laying a finger over her lips. "Shh."

Then he was draining the water from the tub, reaching for a towel. "Stand up."

She obeyed him. He wrapped her up tightly and then gently led her from the bathroom toward the bed.

"Now," he said. "Let's get comfortable."

He arranged the pillows, piling them high and then easing her down onto her back atop them. He lay on his side next to her and began walking his fingers down her arm. "How do you want to be touched right now?"

"Kid gloves," she whispered and his eyes lit with such feverish delight she knew he understood. "Feather fine. Lots and lots and lots of foreplay."

"What? Where? How?"

"Stroke me."

Tentatively, he reached out and with an incredibly light caress grazed the base of his palm over her collarbone.

Callie shivered.

"What else do you like?" he probed.

"Kiss my throat while you're stroking me."

And so he did.

His hand was a silken glide, his lips delicious. He swirled his fingers over her navel. Softly and sweetly he kissed the leaping pulse at her neck.

Short kisses were dropped down the length of her throat, and then tiny succulent nibbles.

She let her head fall back against the pillows. "Go lower."

"With my hands or my mouth?"

"Both."

He dipped his head, trailing his tongue down the middle of her chest to the flat of her sternum before he veered off into other territory. Her nipples beaded hard in greeting.

All the while his lips were finding her breasts, his hand was dancing around the juncture at her thighs. She parted her legs slightly, just enough to let him slip a finger or two between them.

He suckled first one nipple and then the other while strumming her clit lightly with an index finger.

She tilted her pelvis, arched her back. "More," she insisted. "More."

And then his mouth and his fingers were in the same

place and he had moved around so that his head pointed south. His lips closed around the tiny throbbing head of her cleft while his fingers tickled the entrance of her womanhood.

Lacing her fingers around his neck, she muttered "Yes, yes."

She rode the flow of emotions, navigating the swell of pleasure and desire and discovery with accomplished ease. His warmth enveloped and she experienced a sense of safety with him that she'd rarely felt before.

He was lifting her up to a place she'd never known existed. She loved the adventure of him and was fascinated by this aspect of him.

Then she was seized by a sudden bittersweet feeling. This moment could not last. She closed her eyes, determined to ignore the sadness. Besides, this was all she needed. This brief slice of delight. She wasn't a commitment kind of gal. No reason to be sad. She was having fun and he was doing some very nice things with his tongue.

Luke's feet were pressed against the headboard, his long masculine legs parallel to her face. His hard shaft poked into her ribs.

She had a wicked thought. Time he learned about sixty-nine.

Callie turned toward him, curling her spine outward while at the same time shifting her pelvis closer to his mouth and dipping her chin so she could rim the head of him with her tongue.

He gave a yelp of pleased surprised. His mouth was

on her most feminine lips while at the same time she stretched her own mouth over the expansive width of his penis.

His tongue was hot and wet. So was hers.

She swirled. He licked.

Up and down, around and around, they were both moaning and writhing, consumed by pleasure.

On and on they went. He on her, she on him. Licking, sucking, tasting. Glorious sensations rippled through her body, turning her inside out.

They increased the tempo as the pressure built, rising to an inevitable crescendo.

Callie mewled soft whenever he did something right, grunted when he made a wrong move. It didn't take him long to pick up her rhythms, learn what she liked and give her more of it.

She took him deeper until she felt him pressing against the back of her throat, juicy and slick. She rolled her lips back, stretching wider to accommodate his bigness. She wanted to swallow all of him. She breathed in the heady smell of his sex.

Finally, Luke broke away, pulling his mouth from her throbbing anxious clit. "I can't stand it anymore. I have to be inside you."

"Condoms," she gasped, so addled by passion she was impressed that she had remembered. Thank heavens.

"I'm on it," Luke said, swinging his legs off the bed and disappearing into the sitting area. He returned in a matter of seconds with the brown paper sack from the airport, but she was already drifting down from the pinnacle.

"Hang on," he panted, ripping open the box with his

teeth and sending packets of condoms flying around the room. One smacked Callie on her belly.

"Let me." She laughed and peeled open the foil wrapping. He was already in bed again. Callie popped the condom between her teeth and proceeded to use the old "roll the banana" trick on him.

He groaned, took her by the shoulders and flipped her onto her back. He was trembling so hard he could barely mount her.

And then he was inside.

She'd never had a man so thick, filling her up until she feared she might not be able to take any more.

"You're so wet, dripping wet for me."

He was so damned beautiful. Hard, lean, a fine spray of dark hair between his nipples. Her hips twitched against his, the muscles between her thighs clenching almost viciously.

Their breathing changed, getting hoarser, raspier. Their coupling was primal now. Fierce and hungry. He plunged heedlessly into her. Driving them closer and closer to the edge.

They were almost there. Both of them. Ready to come together. As one.

Ah-ah-ah. Callie made a noise, desperate, hungry.

He must have misinterpreted her sound of encouragement and thought she wanted him to hurry when she wanted the exact opposite. He began to pump faster, sliding in and out of her, quickening his rhythm.

Why was he speeding up when they'd been so in sync before? If he kept this up, he was going to go off without her. Half-cocked.

He's too inexperienced to know he's blowing a perfect game.

And then Luke just stopped.

Callie felt as if she'd been left hanging out the open door of a moving car, her hips and butt still suspended on the seat but with her upper body dangling above the roadbed as the asphalt spun away beneath her.

Bizarre sensation.

She realized her shoulders and head had slipped off the bed and she was indeed dangling.

"You're falling." Luke slipped out of her and gently moved her back onto the pillows.

They looked at each other.

"I was going too fast," he said.

She nodded.

"Tell me these things. Don't let me be a bad lover," he pleaded, and the words were bittersweet arrows into her heart.

"Sometimes," she whispered, "it's hard for two people to get used to each other's skin. It takes a while to learn each other. It's not like in the movies."

"Tell me more."

"What about this big guy?" She reached down to cup his burgeoning cock.

"Forget him for now. He survived nine years without your tutelage, he'll survive nine more minutes."

She stroked him but kept talking, low and soothing. "Everyone contains so many familiar ways of making love, of being in their bodies, of being with other people. When a new person comes along who does things differently the strangeness can be something of a shock."

"I shock *you?*" he asked.

"Mister," she said huskily, "you have no idea."

"How do we overcome this strangeness?"

"No way through it…" she started to say.

"Except to do it," he finished for her.

They smiled at each other.

He stroked her chin and the gesture was so tender Callie had an urge to burst into tears. Hormones, she told herself. That's all it was. Instead, she kept talking, ignoring the poignant emotions stirring inside her.

She could not afford to like this guy too much. They had no future together. She had no future with any man. Trouts and Harleys and all that. She was the Midnight Ryder. Callie belonged to the listening public. She had Buck Bryson's time slot. That was all she needed.

Or so she kept telling herself.

Besides, no matter how much Luke wanted her sexually, he really didn't want her for happily-ever-after. She knew this, even if he did not. She was too wild for a controlled man like him. He needed a perky do-gooder who labeled her clothes and put lavender-scented sachets in her panty drawer. He needed a sweet-natured woman who wanted nothing more than to marry him, take care of him and have his babies.

That most decidedly was not her.

Maybe that's what was wrong. They were stuck in this moment. Inwardly, he wanted someone he could make love with, find familiar customs and landmarks with, slide into a future with. Whereas she wanted the opposite. Someone to lose herself in without boundaries. Someone she could slide out of the past with.

And so they were stuck.

Her mind hung in the past; his in the future, the time-less present unfolding into unforeseen depths before them. Here everything was shared. There was nothing to grab hold of and cling onto in the dark except for each other.

So they floated.

Together. On a bed in Orange County, California. Strangers yet intimates. Tentative, searching, scared.

His lips made a gentle connection with hers. Callie sighed into him.

"You're thinking too much," he whispered.

She nodded. It was true.

"Let me take you someplace out of your head."

She spread her legs. "Come inside."

He complied, moving much slower, taking his time. "Callie."

Tears pushed at the back of her eyes. The way he said her name filled her with vulnerability. They were no longer having hot sex. They were truly making love.

That thought would have frozen her stiff if he hadn't been doing all the right things this time, making all the right moves, leading her gently where she so anxiously wanted to go.

Her body vibrated like the steadiness of a plane engine soaring through the clouds. Up he lifted her. Up. Up. Up.

First passion overwhelmed her heart, the hot tears of joy flowing down her cheeks. So long, so long she'd been waiting for this.

For him. The heat spread through her, exploding in a vivid burst of energy.

She heard herself moan, heard him groan as the impact of orgasm gripped him.

His hands shook as he held her torso steady. He thrust into her again and again. His entire being seemed to slide deeper and deeper into hers until she could not differentiate where her body stopped and his began.

Then she felt something earth-shattering. Something she had never experienced before.

It was as if his soul had leaped from his body and shot straight into hers along with his orgasm.

He cried out as his essence poured out of him, imbuing her with streaming currents of his masculine energy.

Together, they melted.

Nothing else existed.

Not Luke the ultraserious bodyguard. Not the sassy, trash-talking Midnight Ryder. Even the room was gone, disappearing in the laser beam moment of blissful orgasmic feeling.

He cried out one last time and shoved himself as deep as he would go into her warmth.

The walls of her sucked at him, gripping, kneading, pulling this man into the very core of her.

Mystical, magical sparks of flesh and fire melded together. Shattering, scattering, torturing. Melting her heart from the inside out.

A second orgasm sprang up from inside her groin, flooded her body, drowning her brain. She was numb, wrung, spent.

Luke's body shuddered as he felt it pour through her. They clung to each other, helpless, as wave after wave of energy rippled through them. Binding them together in one blazing, crazy light of sex before expelling them into the infinite beyond.

Gasping, Luke rolled over, sinking onto his back and taking her with him. He held her close as her chest heaved and quivered.

She slipped her arms around his powerful neck, squeezing him tight as his tears flowed warm and free down his cheeks. And she had the most terrifying feeling that he had given her his heart for safekeeping and she had tucked it irrevocably inside her soul.

11

Luke and Callie lay on their sides facing each other, hands stacked under their heads as they gazed into each other's eyes. An ocean breeze blowing in from the open French doors stirred the top sheet lightly covering their bodies.

"So how'd I do?" he asked.

She grinned at him. "Feeling nervous about your performance?"

"Hell, yes," he admitted. She looked so damned good lying there next to him. Being with her felt good, too.

"Couldn't you tell how much I was enjoying myself?"

"I thought you were enjoying yourself but you could have been faking."

"I don't fake orgasms," she said. "You've been with someone who faked them?"

"Yeah. It doesn't do a whole hell of a lot for the male ego when you find out."

"I can assure you that my orgasm was very real. How about you? How was it for you?"

"Enlightening. I've always wanted to try that technique."

"And now you have."

He laughed and reached for her and pulled her to his chest, the motion inevitable, spontaneous. Her warm sexy breath tickled his neck. "What's next in your bag of tricks?"

She tilted her chin up until their lips were only inches apart and she dropped her voice to a sultry tease. "You'll just have to wait and see."

Luke groaned. "You love torturing me."

"I didn't hear any complaints."

"True."

Moonlight from the balcony fell across Callie's face. She was watching him through heavy-lidded eyes, her pleasure obvious.

"You're so beautiful," he said.

She looked embarrassed at his compliment. "You're not half-bad yourself."

"You look like a different person with your new hair color."

"I feel different. Unfortunately that's not a good thing for my Midnight Ryder persona. Wild hair colors keep me in character." She reached up to touch her hair.

"So how'd you get to be the Midnight Ryder in the first place?"

She chuckled and her face lit up at the memory. "Molly Anne and I cleaned the campus radio station in college. Late one night we were goofing around and we went on the air. Molly Anne pretended to be a caller having sexual problems with her boyfriend. I pretended to be a sex therapist. The phone lines lit up. Dozens of students were calling in. We put on an hour long show before the dean shut us down."

"Bet you were in a lot of trouble."

"We were. Until the next morning when the radio station was deluged with requests for the Midnight Ryder, so they put me on the air." Her impish grin tugged at his heart. Here was a woman who knew how to enjoy herself. He realized how little fun he'd had in his life and how much he liked being around her. This sudden longing for something he'd never had took him completely by surprise.

By nature he was an orderly, structured guy. He preferred to know all the rules before embarking on any task. He had strong views on life and he toiled hard to accomplish good work. But still, somewhere deep inside, he wished he could take himself off the tight, rigid emotional leash that had defined his life.

"So how did you make the leap from college deejay to the big time?" Luke asked.

"The local station in my hometown offered me the gig. Low pay, but boy did I have a good time. Molly Anne was the one busting her hump to get me into bigger markets. We bounced all over the country in the early days but each job was a step up from the last."

"You did it the old-fashioned way. Persistence and hard work."

She nodded. "I paid my fair share of dues. There were many times when Molly Anne and I subsisted on baked potatoes and discount cola. We took in roommates and shopped at Goodwill. But in an odd way it was fun. The spirit of adventure, the naiveté of youth."

"So until this accidental college prank turned career you never thought about going into broadcasting?"

"Oh, no. I was an elementary education major." She shook her head, laughing. "I mean honestly, can you imagine me teaching kindergarten?"

"Actually, I could," he said.

"Get real! I'm too hyperactive for a classroom."

"You're energetic. What better person to teach five-year-olds?"

"And I'm too irreverent."

"That's just another word for perky."

"I couldn't wear miniskirts to work."

He smiled. "You do have world-class legs."

She kissed the end of his nose and giggled. Her light, carefree sound touched something in him.

"You ever think about teaching?"

"But I already do. Every night I teach women how to get in touch with their sexuality."

"No I mean teaching kids like you wanted to do before your life took another route."

"That ship has sailed." She sounded a little wistful. He got the feeling that on some level she wished for a simpler life.

"It does seem you were destined for greatness."

"I wouldn't call this greatness. Fame, acclaim maybe. But greatness? I don't think so."

"Those fans at the airport would disagree with you." Didn't she understand how special she was?

"It's all hype and promotion. Molly Anne's damn good at her job."

"Take some credit, will you? If you weren't so talented, Molly Anne wouldn't have anything to promote."

"Sometimes it feels like such an act. As if I've lost touch with the real me." Her expression turned wistful.

"Who is the real Callie?" he asked, gently stroking the rim of her ear.

"I'm not sure I know. I guess that's why I'm so into fantasy fulfillment," she said softly and his heart beat harder. "If I'm living a fantasy, I don't have to face reality."

There were plenty of times he wished he could escape into fantasy, but he was too much of a realist. Perhaps that was why he'd never been able to relax and play in the bedroom.

Until now. Until tonight with Callie.

The memory of what they'd just shared, how he'd dared to let his guard down with her caused his blood to run hot, but it also reminded him to stay cautious. No matter how much fun he'd had with her, she'd made it perfectly clear it could never be more than just enjoyable sex.

I can do this. I can separate emotions from sex. I can have fun within the perimeters of our arrangement without needing anything more from her.

"You're thinking too hard. Stop thinking so hard." She pressed the pad of her thumb against his forehead and smoothed out the wrinkles that had settled between his brows.

"Huh?"

"I've noticed that about you. When you have something on your mind you get this intense look on your face. Wanna talk about it?"

He shook his head. "I want to kiss you."

"Do you really want to kiss me or are you just trying to avoid talking about your feelings?"

"Both," he admitted, a little disconcerted that she'd pegged him so accurately.

"So tell me what's on your mind. Tell me what you're feeling."

Luke's chest tightened. He was ill at ease with the thought of sharing himself with a woman he barely knew. He didn't know how to handle this or the look of expectancy shining in her sweet brown eyes so he did what any red-blooded man would do when cornered by a woman to discuss his emotions. He went into default mode and took control.

He took her hand, guided it to his erection and said, "This is what's on my mind."

LUKE REACHED FOR HER in the wee hours of the morning. In the muzziness of predawn. Callie was still half-asleep, not sure if she was dreaming or if he was really pressing his urgent body against her buttocks. She turned to see his dark head burrowed deep within her pillow, his eyes closed, their bodies lightly covered with the sheet.

He wanted it three times in one night? The guy was insatiable.

Was he asleep? Was she?

Reaching up, he fingered her hair. "Nice," he murmured. "I like this. The real you."

Something grabbed Callie's heart and squeezed. Sorrow? Remorse? How could he say that when he didn't even know the real her?

He's dreaming, she assured herself. *So are you. Just go with it.*

He pulled her across his body, the sheet sliding down her buttocks.

"Straddle me," he whispered, and so she did, her body still aching sweetly from their previous love-making.

She was surprised at how slick she was, how easily she slid down over him. She rocked her pubic bone against his. In this somnambulant state she could let herself care deeply for him. Anything she felt right now did not count. It was all fantasy.

Right?

She rode him as the sun begin to creep around the edges of the curtains, as the ocean crashed against the shore, as her heart filled with an emotion she'd never experienced.

He pitched his hips upward, thrusting against her, every muscle inside him clenched. He brushed his thumbs across her jutting nipples. Callie threw her head back, quickened the pace. Rocking, riding, shaking the rafters.

The strum of desire coiled tighter and tighter inside her center. The climax swept through her, as hard as it was sudden, bucking her body over his, stretching her dream to the breaking point.

She called his name as she came, stunned and overcome by this man. This virtual stranger. The potency of him compelled her so completely.

He grasped her tight as his release shot through him a few seconds later and then she fell heavily against his chest.

Breathing hard, he slipped her into the curve of his

arms and just as she drifted back to sleep, Callie wondered if Luke had worn a condom.

"I SCREWED UP," Luke confessed, tucking the cell phone under his chin. He was pacing the short balcony, the drapes partially open. If he tilted his head he could see Callie's beautiful bare bottom where she was lying stretched out on the bed.

Sleeping. Sated.

He smiled in spite of himself, remembering. He couldn't help it. He had taken her, made her his own.

And there lay the crux of the problem. He was already claiming her when he had no business thinking of her as his. He had promised her that he would not fall in love with her. He had promised himself.

"You?" Zack hooted. "Mr. Paragon of Virtue? I don't believe it. How did you screw up?"

"I violated the code."

"You slept with Callie."

"How did you guess?"

"How could I not? I can't think of anything else that would torture you enough to phone me at 7 a.m. West Coast time on a Sunday morning unless you had gotten her killed."

"No." Luke ran a hand along his jaw. "She's very much alive."

"So stop beating yourself up. You had sex with her. It's about time you had sex with someone."

"It's not the only mistake I made."

"No?"

Luke swallowed. "I think I forgot to use a condom."

"There is no think. You either used one or you didn't."

"We were barely awake. Maybe we were asleep. Maybe I was dreaming. I used one the first time. Even the second. But the third time, we...I..."

Shit. How could he have done something so completely irresponsible?

"Don't panic. She's probably using birth control. A savvy woman like Callie Ryder."

"You're probably right." Luke nodded, trying hard to convince himself. There couldn't be a pregnancy from this. There simply could not. He would not have a repeat of what had happened with Rachel.

Unexpected pressure burned at the back of his eyes. He'd been a stupid kid then. He'd had an excuse. This time there was no excuse. None at all. He had messed up. Badly.

What if Callie got pregnant?

A soft mushy feeling expanded in his heart. He would love to be a dad. But at the right time. With the right woman. A woman who wanted to be a mother.

But that wasn't what Callie wanted. She had made it perfectly clear she wasn't interested in a long-term relationship. She had a huge career ahead of her. He didn't fit in with her plans of stardom and Luke knew it.

Then you just better pray she's not pregnant.

"Luke?" Zack said. "You still there?"

"I'm still here."

"What else is bothering you?"

Luke took a deep breath. He didn't like talking about his feelings but this boulder was too heavy to shoulder alone. "I have feelings for her."

"What kind of feelings?"

"You know what kind of feelings."

"You're telling me you're in love with her? But you just met her, man."

"I don't know. I can't explain it."

"Calm down. You've just had some phenomenal sex. That'll get almost any guy thinking lovey-dovey thoughts. And there's that element of danger. You know full well danger and excitement can skew a man's view of reality."

Luke nodded. That was true.

"You're not in love with her," Zack reassured him. "You haven't known her long enough to fall in love. It's simple chemistry and that bodyguard-protectee thing you got going on. Trust me, the feeling will pass."

"Have you ever felt this for someone you were hired to protect?"

"Yes. It happens to all bodyguards at least once in their careers. Hey, look at it this way. You got it out of your system on your first assignment."

Luke blew out his breath and threaded a hand through his hair. Zack was right. He had to be right. Because he simply could not be falling in love with Callie Ryder.

"Momma?" Callie whispered softly into the phone.

Luke was out on the balcony and she didn't want him to overhear her conversation. She was under the covers, staring at the packet of birth control pills. She'd fished them from her purse the minute she'd woken up and re-membered about last night.

The peach-colored packet with the extra pill in the

row. The one she'd apparently forgotten to take between the hubbub of hectic travel and the terror of almost getting creamed by a drunken stalker in a dark sedan.

And having fabulous sex with Luke.

"Hello, honey." Hearing her mother's voice instantly made her feel better. "I was wondering when you were gonna get around to calling and telling me about the Harley."

"He's not a Harley, Mom."

"They're *all* Harleys, Callie."

"And all women are trout?"

"Yes. In a manner of speaking. Swimming along, minding their own businesses, absolutely no need for transportation. What do you wanna go messing with a Harley for, Cal?"

"How come we're not catfish or perch or bass? How come guys are not Ducatis or Hondas or Suzukis? Why Harleys?"

"What other names are Harleys known by?"

"Hogs."

"You've got it."

"Then why don't you just say a woman needs a man like a trout needs a hog?"

"Stop being a smart aleck. When were you going to tell me that you decided to do something dreadful like getting engaged?"

"Luke and I are not engaged."

"What's wrong with just sleeping with him or living with him if you must, but marriage? I thought I taught you better than that."

"Not every guy is like Dad and you're not listening to me. We are not engaged."

"The *Celebrity Insider* says you are."

"Well, they're wrong. It's just a cover story that Molly Anne cooked up for publicity purposes. Luke's my bodyguard while I'm on tour."

"Oh." Her mother paused in her rant. "Well then, that's okay. Wait a minute, why do you need a bodyguard?"

"Because some weirdo has been making death threats against me. He claims he doesn't like the sexy messages I'm feeding young women."

Momma snorted. "Just like a man."

"Can we not indulge in guy bashing for two minutes, please?"

"You're right." Her mother settled down a little. "I do get carried away on the subject of Harleys."

It had been fifteen years and her mother still hadn't gotten over being betrayed by Callie's dad. Callie wished her mother wasn't so soured on the entire gender.

Callie peeped out from under the covers and cast a lingering look at the balcony. Luke was still out there on his cell phone from the sound of it. Some of those Harleys weren't half bad.

"I'm glad you hired a bodyguard and didn't let that creep stop you from touring."

"You didn't raise a coward."

"No, I didn't." She sounded proud. "And here I am getting so flustered about that engagement nonsense I've forgotten the important part. Congratulations, honey, on your promotion. I'm so proud of you. You set out to do something and you did it. And you made it in a man's world at that. You do such a needed service. Educating young women about the power of their sexuality. You teach them to hold their heads high and be proud of who they are. You're something special, Cal gal, you know that?"

Her stomach fluttered at her mother's words. Any fleeting thoughts she had about not taking Buck Bryson's time slot instantly disappeared. How could she not accept the job when it was offered to her? It would make her mother so proud.

She would completely embrace the Midnight Ryder. It was who she had become, after all. She couldn't throw away all her hard work. Not even if it meant throwing away the last shred of the self she used to be.

"I love you, Momma."

"Love you, too, honey."

Just as she hung up, Callie felt a tap on her shoulder. Callie wormed out from under the covers to find Luke standing over her, smiling. And he was gloriously naked.

Now that's a man I wouldn't mind waking up to every morning.

Damn. She had to stop thinking things like that.

"You were out on the balcony in the nude?"

"It's 7 a.m. on a Sunday morning at a beach resort hotel. No one's up."

"And here I thought you embarrassed easily."

"After last night?" His eyes were laughing. "You gotta be kidding."

"Wanna order room service?" she asked, flipping over to sit up. She was feeling strangely modest this morning and pulled the covers up over her breasts.

"I thought maybe we could talk first."

"Oh, okay." She scooted over to the middle of the bed. "Have a seat."

He sank down on the edge. She wondered how he would look if he let his hair grow out. The military cut was a little severe.

"Speaking of last night," he said.

His insecurity was endearing. His eyes searched her face as he waited for her to pass judgment on his performance. He looked so strong and yet at the same time so incredibly vulnerable. Smiling wistfully, she reached out and traced her fingers over his lips.

"Last night," she said. "Was wonderful. You were way more than okay. How was it for you?"

"Last night was like my birthday, Christmas Eve and the Fourth of July all wrapped up in one awesome package. But what I wanted to discuss was the last time we had sex."

"When you were so sleepy you forgot to use a condom."

Callie drew her knees up to her chest and studied him. "Yeah."

"If you're worried about AIDS, my doctor does a test on me every year as a precaution. I advocate safe sex on my show and I want to set a good example. I can prove I'm HIV negative and I have no other sexually transmitted diseases."

"It's not that," he said.

"You're worried about birth control?"

He nodded.

"I'm on the pill. Don't worry." She waved a hand.

Callie couldn't say why she didn't tell him she'd missed taking yesterday's pill. Maybe because she didn't consider it his problem.

"That's good." He sat there nodding with a faraway look in his eyes. "That's real good."

There was an awkward silence.

"I was worried about that," he said at last.

"Is there something you want to tell me?"

"I can't believe I made the same mistake twice. I mean here I am celibate for nine years and I was so certain that when I had sex again it would be with someone that I was in love with and…"

He was having a hard time with this. Callie just sat waiting patiently letting him say what he had to say at his own pace.

"Uh-huh," she murmured encouragingly.

"I got a girl pregnant," he finally blurted. "Her name was Rachel Delong. She was the hottest thing in high school. She had a reputation, if you know what I mean. We were at a party. We were drunk. We spent the night together on a pool table in some guy's basement. It was just hot sex. Fun. It was supposed to be no strings attached, no complications. That's what she told me. I was horny and seventeen. I thought, why not?"

Callie was honored that he trusted her enough to tell her all this. It choked her up inside.

"I had a condom. We used it. Then we fell asleep. The next morning, she wakes me up and we go at it again but we don't have any more condoms. We were both too worked up to stop."

Callie had the strongest urge to reach out, pat his

shoulder and tell him it was okay. He was young. He made a mistake but she didn't want to trivialize his pain. He was still hurting. She could see it in his face.

"When Rachel told me she was pregnant I offered to marry her. I didn't love her but I wanted that kid...."

She could hear the unshed tears in his throat and her heart wrenched for the seventeen-year-old Luke had once been. She thought of her own pregnancy scare with Chip Mancuso and swallowed hard. She knew something of what he had gone through. She wondered how different things might have been for her if it had been Luke she'd known in high school instead of Chip.

For the first time since he started talking, Luke met her gaze. "Rachel had an abortion. There was nothing I could do to change her mind, so I went with her to the clinic, held her hand while she waited her turn and then I sat in the lobby until it was over. That's when I swore I wasn't ever going to have unprotected casual sex again. Last night, I broke that vow with you."

"Oh, Luke, you were a kid. It was a long time ago. A bad mistake."

She could have told him about her own mistake. About Chip and her pregnancy scare. It might have made him feel better, knowing he wasn't alone.

But she just couldn't bring herself to tell him. Sharing intimacies led to a stronger bond. And a strong bond led to deeper feelings. And deeper feelings led to strings and attachments and she just couldn't handle that. Because she knew if she was not very, very careful Luke Cardasian was going to break her heart.

"Did I make a bad mistake with you, Callie?" he asked.

"No, oh no." He looked so tortured she was glad she had not told him about the missed pill. She cupped his face in her hands. "It was beautiful. You're beautiful. One of these days you will find the love of your life. You will have those kids you want. But until then there's nothing wrong with enjoying your life and honoring your sexuality."

"But I forgot to use a condom."

"No harm done. We'll just be extra careful from now on."

"We're going to keep having sex?"

"Aren't we?"

"Um…I don't know if it's such a good idea."

What was she going to say? Tell him last night was a huge mistake? That it had been a one-time deal and they needed to back off. That now they would spend the rest of the trip jammed in close quarters but not touching or kissing or making love.

Not damned likely.

"We obviously have chemistry. There's something going on between us. Why torture ourselves? Just as long as we keep things light and keep the condoms handy, we'll be fine."

But therein lay the rub. Keeping it light.

He wasn't the kind of guy who took a woman to bed and then sneaked out in the middle of the night. His feet were solidly rooted to the floor.

And *that* scared her more than anything.

She'd never been around a guy with staying power. She was good at chasing men off. She didn't know what to do with one who refused to budge.

12

BLEARY FROM LACK OF SLEEP, Luke and Callie, along with Molly Anne, took off for the next stop on their itinerary, cruising up the Pacific Coast Highway in a limo to Santa Barbara.

Molly Anne and Callie sat in the back while Luke sat facing them on the opposite seat. He'd been acting pleasant but distant ever since they'd left their hotel suite. Callie supposed she'd been acting that way, too. Something monumental had happened to them last night. Monumental and disturbing and neither one of them wanted to discuss it.

So they pretended nothing had happened. Luke and Molly Anne had been mapping out the details for Callie's security needs but she was too keyed up to concentrate on what they were saying. She restlessly tapped her foot against the floorboard.

Molly Anne looked up at her. "You okay?"

"Fine."

"Are you nervous because Roger hasn't called to officially offer you Buck's time slot yet?"

"No."

To be honest she hadn't even thought about Roger or Buck Bryson and his morning slot. The only thing dominating her thoughts was what had happened last night. Callie shot a look across the car at Luke but quickly glanced away. She didn't want Molly Anne tuning in to the tension between them.

"Don't worry. I'm certain Roger will be calling you soon."

"I'm not worried."

"Then why are your hands clenched? Do you need a Valium?"

"I'm fine, dammit," Callie snapped.

"Oookay," Molly Anne said and raised her palms. "Forget I asked. Just trying to be helpful."

Why was she acting so testy? What was the matter with her?

Before she had time to puzzle out the true source of her irritability, Molly Anne's cell phone rang. She peeked at the caller ID then grinned at Callie. "It's Roger."

A momentary panic clutched Callie's stomach. If Roger offered her the position was she going to take it? She glanced over at Luke again. He had dark shades on and he wasn't smiling. He looked totally enigmatic. What was he thinking?

"Roger," Molly Anne purred into the cell phone. "Good morning. Yes, she's right here."

And the next thing Callie knew she was talking to Roger.

"Callie, I suppose you've heard we let Buck Bryson go," Roger said.

"Un-huh." Her chest tightened with dread.

"It's no secret that *Let's Talk About Sex* is KSXX's most successful program."

"Yes." Her fingers tightened on Molly Anne's cell phone. She could feel Luke watching her from beneath the shades that shielded his emotions.

"We want to take you into Buck's slot and retitle the show, *Let's Talk About Last Night*. The format will encourage callers to phone up and share their sexy adventures from the night before."

"Provocative concept," Callie said, doing her best to sound noncommittal.

"We'll keep your name the same. Even though you will no longer be on at midnight, you'll be discussing midnight fantasies the morning after."

"No name change?" No chance for a new identity.

"The board wants it that way. They want you to stay the same."

"Oh." This was it. Her last chance out. Her last opportunity to walk away.

"So what do you say? The job comes with a raise." Then Roger named a figure that took her breath.

Molly Anne was grinning and crossed her fingers. Her oldest friend was counting on her. Barb, too. Her mother was proud of her accomplishments and she would be proving something to her father. How could she turn this offer down?

And what about Luke?

She angled him a sidelong glance. What did he think?

It didn't matter what he thought. He didn't figure into her life in the slightest.

Why then was she so worried about looking into his eyes? He took off his sunglasses and their gazes met.

"Callie?" Roger asked. "You still there? Did I lose you?"

"You didn't lose me, Roger."

"So what's your answer?"

Should I take the job? Callie silently asked Luke with her eyes.

Slowly, he shook his head. *Not my place to tell you what to do.*

It was weird that she knew exactly what he was thinking but she knew they had no chance of a future together. He was too constrained for her and she was too rebellious for him.

"Roger," she said, still meeting Luke's eyes dead-on. "I'll take the job."

Was it her imagination, or did Luke seem disappointed.

MOLLY ANNE WAS supercharged after Callie accepted Roger's offer. They checked in at another beachside resort hotel in Santa Barbara and immediately Molly Anne whisked her off to lunch with a local journalist followed by two back-to-back book signings. Her friend buzzed with excitement, while Callie, dazed from having accepted Buck's time slot when she didn't even want it, signed book after book.

Following the signings, she was the scheduled guest of honor in the radio booth at a local arts-and-craft fair. Callie smiled and nodded and greeted fans until she thought her mouth was going to crack from so much smiling. Like any good bodyguard, Luke blended anonymously into the background, but he was always there. Her silent protector.

He made her feel warm and safe. Which, in itself, was disconcerting. She'd grown up fast and learned to take care of herself at an early age. She'd met life head-on. She wasn't accustomed to being sheltered.

To shake the emotions she could not encourage, she focused instead on the physical. On how he'd made her body feel. On what she planned to do to him once they were back in the hotel room.

It was such fun thinking up sexy scenarios for them to act out and a great way to get through the hectic day.

By the time all the events were over, Callie was trembling with anticipation. She had a fantasy in mind she'd always wanted to try.

It was nearly midnight by the time they got back to the resort.

"You tired?" she asked him as Luke punched the up button for the elevator. Molly Anne's room was accessed by a different bank of elevators and they'd already parted company with her.

"Exhausted," he confessed. "You wore me out last night."

"I'm so revved up from all the excitement I couldn't sleep if I tried," Callie admitted.

He arched an eyebrow. "You have something in mind?"

She didn't want to give away her plan, not so soon, but she baited the trap. "I think I'll go work out in the gym. Since you're so tired, why don't you go on to bed?"

"You're not going down there alone," he said. "Besides, I need a good workout, too."

"I was hoping you'd say that." She grinned.

They went to their room and changed into workout

clothes. Luke wore a black muscle shirt and gray cotton shorts. Callie had on black Lycra shorts and a black sports bra. They used their key card to get into the gym. As Callie had hoped, at this hour the place was empty.

She carried her gym bag through the cardio area filled with treadmills and recumbent bikes and stair climbers and walked into the weight room beyond. She dropped the gym bag next to a leg press machine. Luke followed her inside. He picked up two twenty-five pound barbells and seated himself on the weight bench.

As Callie worked out on the leg press, she kept sneaking surreptitious glances over at Luke. He was doing bicep curls, his concentration focused on performing slow, steady repetitions.

In, out, in, out. The weights clanged gently as she pushed with her thighs.

Luke was a glory to watch. Toned and hard and leanly muscled. His pecs flexed and rippled beneath the tight fit of his muscle shirt and Callie's heart got snagged up in her throat. The small gym was suddenly very hot in spite of the cool air blasting through the air-conditioning vents.

With each exertion he expelled his breath in short, rhythmic exhalations. It was a rough, sexy noise that caused her nipples to pucker beneath the snugness of her sports bra.

His shirt dampened with sweat. His tantalizing pheromones enticed her. She craved the smell of him beyond all reason. It was a creatural impulse that made her feel connected to him, to nature, to her sensuality.

He lay with his back flat against the weight bench

and did overhead presses with the barbells, his long lean body gleaming with perspiration.

Callie licked her lips.

When she could stand it no longer, she got up, stepped over and straddled his body on the weight bench. She hovered above his knees. Up went the barbells. Down went her hand, boldly touching his cock.

"What are you doing?" He stared at her, clearly aghast.

"Teaching you the joys of spontaneous, semipublic sex."

"But we're in the weight room of a resort gym. A hotel guest could walk in on us at any minute."

"Not likely. It's after midnight on a Monday. Besides, the possibility of someone walking in on us is sort of the point," she said. "Anyway, we don't have to get all the way naked."

"What do you mean?" he asked hoarsely and dropped the weights.

They plunked loudly to the floor. He might be protesting but the expression in his eyes told Callie he was intrigued.

She leaned over and pulled the gym bag toward her. Then she reached inside and pulled out a pair of scissors, along with a condom, and then handed him the scissors.

"What do you want me to do with these?"

"Cut the crotch out of my shorts."

Callie hadn't expected him to attack the task with such glee. The way he grabbed her inseam, pulled down and started snipping away caused her to giggle. Funny, she wasn't a giggler. But ever since meeting Luke she seemed to giggle all the time. Her mission might have been to teach him a few things about sex, but here he was, teaching her a few new things about herself.

"Clip the strap on my G-string thong, too," she instructed once she felt the air hit her bare skin where he'd cut a perfect diamond shape out of the Lycra.

"You're a bossy thing."

"And don't you forget it," she teased.

Luke snipped her underwear off, then tossed the scissors on the floor beside the barbells. He raised his shoulders up off the weight bench, banded one arm around her bottom and pulled her down with him. He snuggled her against the rigid length of him. His grip held her tight; she squirmed but he wasn't about to let her go. "Who's in charge now?"

She was lying directly on top of him on the narrow weight bench. Torturously, he pushed her bra up and fitted his mouth over her pert nipple and his deep groan of appreciation matched her own.

Her hips twitched against his pelvis; the muscles between her thighs clenched hungrily. He reached for her breasts with his hands but she grabbed his wrists and pinned them above his head.

"No hands," she commanded.

He made a guttural sound of despair. "What do you have up your sleeve?"

"Just wait and see."

Luke swore.

"Go ahead. Talk dirty. It turns me on."

She reached down and freed his burgeoning erection

through the opening in his workout shorts. His whole body jerked. Most exciting was the part of him that jerked hard against her inner thigh. With one hand still pinning his wrists in place over his head, she ducked her head and gently nipped one of his nipples through the thin material of his muscle shirt.

He gasped and writhed and swore again.

Callie licked her way up his body, his chin and his jaw and his earlobe. When she raised her head, she discovered he was staring at her with a gaze so blazingly hot she felt as if she'd been singed.

The idea that they were making out in the weight room and that any minute someone could walk in on them was beyond thrilling. It was dangerous, yes, but that's what made it all the more arousing. The pulse in his wrist leaped hard and fast and she knew he was just as turned on as she was, if not more so.

She loved how quickly she was loosening him up, how swiftly he was learning to read her. She had to give credit where credit was due. Luke was an apt pupil.

Now all she had to do was push him over the edge, make him totally lose control.

She grabbed for the condom she'd left on the edge of the weight bench. Using her teeth, she tore the foil packet open, extracted the rubber and then shifted so she could roll it onto him.

Sighing, she sank down on the length of him and let go of his wrists in the process. Immediately, he spanned her waist with his hands, holding her in place and hissing out his breath on a long exhalation.

He was inside her. It felt as though they were both

inside the same skin or a great mysterious cave. "Ride me hard. Give me all you've got, hold nothing back."

And so she did, riding him hard and fast until they were flying as you might fly in a dream. High. She was so high with passion, so full of him. No one had ever stirred her like this.

They were floating together in a vastness of sensation and every blissful inch felt right and good and true. Callie didn't know who was inside whom. They were both inside. There was no outside. They occupied the universe and spun in it together.

The delicious expanse of their oneness spread and grew and swelled. A sweet, silent supernova twirling faster than the speed of light across the space of their own rapturous interior. They bathed in the white heat of their joining until the last bit of energy was drained from their bodies and they tumbled wide-eyed and breathless back down into a world of gleaming metal, leather benches and heavy weights.

They had gone so far together, had shared so much intimacy that when they came back into their separate selves, a soft sadness took over.

The experience had been so awe inspiring, so otherworldly that Callie did not know how to act with Luke. From the expression on his face, she could tell he felt just as awkward as she did.

They did not know each other well enough. They had no familiar ground, no safe place in which to reclaim their separate identities. In the confines of that little gym they were in uncharted territory.

A sense of loss set in. As though they'd stolen each

other's souls. Suddenly Callie realized she was frightened. More frightened than she'd been in a very long time. Quickly, she got up, reached into her gym bag and pulled a pair of baggy sweatpants up over her now crotchless shorts.

And then Luke did something that touched her heart. He reached out and took her hand.

THEY HELD HANDS all the way back to their room. He knew he had a goofy grin on his face but he did not want it wiped off. Luke fitted the key card into the lock, then turned to playfully lift Callie, gym bag and all, into his arms.

He was so addled from what they'd shared, so uncharacteristically playful, that he forgot to be cautious. She was laughing and his heart was soaring. The door snapped closed behind them and he carried her toward the bed without ever realizing something was terribly wrong.

Later, Luke would castigate himself for letting his guard down for even one tiny second. He'd done something that he'd never done before. He had allowed sex to cloud his judgment.

Just as he was about to toss Callie on the bed, she gasped. "Omigod, Luke, no."

His hands curled tightly around her as his gaze welded on the dead bird with a broken neck placed strategically on the turned-down sheets. Callie brought her hands up to cover her eyes.

Luke swung around, determined to get her away from the awful sight. When he turned he saw the ugly message emblazoned across the mirror of the bureau in Callie's scarlet lipstick.

You're next.

AFTER FINDING the dead bird, Luke had fled the room with Callie and taken her to spend the night with Molly Anne. He'd contacted the Santa Barbara police and spent several hours answering their questions. They dusted for fingerprints but most everything in the room had been wiped clean.

On advice from the police, he changed Callie's itinerary in case the stalker had obtained access to her schedule. They were supposed to have caught a plane for San Francisco and she'd been slated to speak at a local university. He rescheduled her speaking engagement, canceled his and Callie's airplane tickets and rented a car. Then he made a special trip to an all-night sporting goods store.

The following morning he sent Molly Anne on ahead to arrange additional security for their stay in San Francisco and make reservations at a different hotel under assumed names. Then he and Callie took off up PCH 1 in a black PT Cruiser convertible.

He tossed her the package he'd picked up at the sporting goods store the night before.

"What's this?" she asked.

"It's for you."

"A present? Oh, Luke, how sweet."

"It's not a present," he said, suddenly wishing he had gotten her something nice. Like flowers or candy or some racy underwear.

She opened the small package. "Lipstick?"

"No, the lipstick case is a disguise."

Callie turned it around in her hand. "Oh. Ultra-strength mace."

"I thought you needed something to protect yourself with," he said gruffly.

"That's so thoughtful of you. And in this adorable lipstick case, too." She leaned over, the seat belt pulled against her breasts and gave him a one-armed hug. "But why do I need mace when I have you."

"You had me with you last night and someone still managed to break into our room and threaten you."

"It's not your fault, Luke."

He glanced over at her. She was wearing a pair of smart denim shorts that showed off a mile of tanned legs and a sexy leopard-print halter top. She'd settled back into her seat but he could still smell the intoxicating scent of her on his clothes. "It's my job to protect you. I didn't do my job last night."

"Hey, nothing happened to me and besides, I distracted you."

"I shouldn't have let myself become distracted." He clenched his jaw.

"Don't be so hard on yourself."

He gripped the steering wheel tightly. "Maybe we should call this whole thing off."

"What whole thing?"

"This you-giving-me-sex-lessons thing."

"It's not going to stop you from being distracted," Callie pointed out. "If anything you'll be even more distracted, wanting to make love to me and yet keeping me off-limits."

She was right. He sighed. "Then the smart thing would be for me to take myself off the case and find you another bodyguard."

"I don't want another bodyguard. I want you."

"Yeah, well, I'm not doing a very good job of keeping you safe."

"Luke, lighten up." She ran a hand across his brow. "You know what I think?

"You should give yourself a day off. We should get a picnic, hit the beach, have some fun on the way up to San Fran. You canceled my appointments until tomorrow afternoon."

It was tempting. He would love nothing more than seeing her frolicking in the ocean surf in a bikini. He shook his head.

"Please? For me? To tell you the truth, I need a break from all this notoriety. It's starting to get to me." The pleading look in her eyes got to him. Why couldn't he ever say no to her?

"All right," he conceded. "But only for a few hours and only on one condition."

"What's that?" she asked.

"You never leave my side."

"Deal," she said and stuck out a hand.

He shook her hand, but he couldn't help wondering if he was making another horrible mistake.

13

THEY STOPPED for a picnic lunch at a secluded beach. Callie had stripped off her top and shorts to reveal the string bikini Luke had been fantasizing about seeing her wear.

Did the woman have any idea how she was driving him crazy? From the way she strutted down the beach, yeah, she had a damned good idea what she was doing. She moved ahead of him, searching for the best picnic spot. He trailed behind, surveying the area, making sure they had not been followed.

The sun was warm on his skin, the ocean spray salty against his tongue. Watching Callie's bottom twitch as she strode through the sand, experiencing his desire for her rising fresh and hard made Luke feel as if he was a one-cell animal, responding to every stimulus he encountered. Everything about her was erotic. The sway of her hips, the jut of her breasts, the sight of her pecan-blond hair tousled by the breeze.

She found a nice spot, cloaked from the prying eyes of any passersby that might stray over. He liked the area. It was secure as any place on a public beach. Bending at the waist, she spread out the blanket she carried and plunked down onto the sand.

Luke sank to the ground beside her, settled the bag of submarine sandwiches that they'd picked up at a drive-through and a couple of bottled sodas between them. He watched as she unwrapped the sandwiches and the smell of pickles and lunch meat made him salivate.

But it wasn't just the smell of food invigorating his salivary glands.

Every whim of Callie's body triggered the hairs on his wrist to quiver. Every vagary of sunlight dappling across her sumptuous body registered sharp and vivid on his retina. Sensation after sensation washed over him like ocean waves. Nothing was lost in translation.

His senses were on high alert, his body tuned for trouble. He would not let anything happen to Callie. He would lay his life on the line for her without thinking twice.

She looked at him with an unusual light in her eyes. It startled him and he appraised her, trying to decipher what was going on inside her head. His body took stock of the world, of this moment, like an intense and vigilant general moving through an intricate battlefield, searching for configurations and subterfuge.

The novelty of her, the surprise of the expression she was giving him riveted Luke.

They watched each other as they ate their sandwiches and washed them down with sodas. They didn't talk. They just sat quietly enjoying each other, enjoying the time away from Callie's hectic schedule. Savoring the respite from danger.

After they'd finished eating, Callie reached out to touch his shoulder. His skin came alive underneath her fingers.

"Make love to me, Luke."

He should say no. He wanted to say no. To be strong and in control. But one sweeping glance at her body encased so provocatively in that string bikini and he never stood a chance. He opened his arms and in an instant, she was at his side, kissing him thirstily.

Relishing the sensation of her mouth against his, Luke threaded his fingers through her hair, held her close and felt the steady beating of her heart.

Life had taught him to be guarded. His parents had taught him to be strong and in control. It was difficult for him to allow his emotions to override his instincts of self-preservation and allow her to see his vulnerabilities.

She astonished him. Not only by her stunning uniqueness but also by the way she made him feel unique. He confronted the novelty of what was happening inside him, acknowledging it at the same time realizing it couldn't last.

But for the moment, their energies were merged, looming bright, edges jagged, the details ravishing. Kissing her, caressing her body with the flats of his palms was a sensory litany.

With expert movements, she reached for the waistband of his pants.

Luke kicked off his boots, unbuckled his belt.

He wanted her more than he wanted to breathe, but Luke suddenly felt bereft and could not really explain why. He appreciated her mastery of sex and longed for her to teach him everything she knew. But once he achieved mastery, once he knew both her body and his own inside out, he would lose this achingly sweet superawareness. He would lose the innocence of a beginner.

He knew now why he'd waited so long to fully explore his sexuality. He'd been afraid that once the novelty wore off, once he'd learned everything he needed to know, there would be no surprises left. And for a man who lived by a disciplined code, part of him ached for the freshness of discovery.

It was time to let go of those fears. Time to understand there was something valuable in experience. Time to realize there was always something new to learn, always fresh insights to be gained. His life did not have to pass in a comfortable blur as he feared it would if he hadn't joined the navy, gone to Limbasa, avoided true intimacy.

Callie helped him understand these things. She lived on her senses, thrived on her sensuality. She wasn't ashamed or embarrassed or limited by other peoples' views. She wasn't lazy about life. She lived with a sense of marvel, with that extra dose of verve that escaped the general populace. She gorged herself on life and he wanted to be part of her feast.

She undid his fly and stripped off his pants. He flung off his shirt and lay back down. She knelt beside him and traced her fingers over his belly.

Their senses combined, expanded. Taste, sight, smell, sound, touch became a cavalcade of experience. He tasted the saltiness of their pooled flavors. He saw how the sun picked up flecks of gold in her hair. He smelled the sweet richness of her femininity. He heard her raspy, excited breathing. His fingers tingled with the feel of her smooth, satiny skin.

She moaned softly when he cupped her breasts and

his erection grew stiffer. During their sex play she produced a condom and helped him put it on.

He liked his body when he was with her. It felt as new to him as hers did. His muscles seemed stronger, his nerves more alive. He loved her body. What it did. How she responded. He liked the way her back arched when he touched her behind the knees. He loved the way she purred when he skimmed his hands over just the right spots. He thrilled to knead his fingertips along her spine, loved to explore her bones and make her tremble.

Again and again and again he kissed her, aiming for this or that. Her chin, her cheeks, her nose. Her navel, her elbow, her toes. He stroked her and gently touched her parting flesh.

Luke felt powerless and exposed, shaking with emotion, desperate to be merged with her. He coiled around her, tracing his quivering hands over her body, mapping every part of her that he could touch—her freckles, the little valley between her nose and her lips, the faint dusky network of veins beneath her pale softness. Luxuriant curves and elegant bones. Sturdy, agile muscles. A miracle of nature, holding him with all her potency, delighting him with her skill.

She pulled his erection with long, lazy, caressing strokes until he was harder than he had ever been in his life.

Then unexpectedly, always unexpectedly, he could always expect unexpectedly with Callie, she flipped over onto all fours on the blanket.

"Take me from behind," she commanded.

Luke hissed in his breath, the stimulus of seeing her

bare fanny in the air was more than he could withstand. He rose up on his knees, spanned her waist with his hands and claimed her.

"More," she pleaded. "I need more of you."

He sank deeper, joining their bodies. Vibrant impulses shot through him. His body seemed to double inside. He was under her skin and she was under his. Literally and emotionally.

"Harder," she said. "Faster. Give me everything, Luke, everything."

He obeyed because he was helpless to do anything else. There on the beach, hidden by vegetation, the ocean breeze blowing against his naked skin, the rushing sound of the sea in his ears, he gave it all up.

Her body sheathed his. He hid himself inside her. He disappeared from view and he was not scared. She opened up her internal workings to him. He added his organ to hers and it was as if it was meant to be there all along.

And as they came together in one gigantic overwhelming simultaneous orgasm, Luke realized he'd taken the ultimate risk.

AFTER SAN FRANCISCO the cities began to run together. Portland, Seattle, Las Vegas, Phoenix. The fans' faces changed and blurred into an amalgamation of eager, young twenty-somethings desperately looking to Callie to sort out their love lives for them. Everything blended into a routine process. There were no more stalker threats. Everything was the same.

Except the nights with Luke.

The following nights passed in a glorious blaze of sexual discovery. Callie alternated between teaching her lover how to please her and learning all she could about his delectable body.

And even though they did not hear anything more from the stalker, Luke stayed on alert, never letting his guard down when they were in public. After what had happened outside Madigan's he didn't like her to go out at night. Not that she minded. Callie was all for staying in. Their room service bill was astronomical, but ah, the creative things they did with food.

She liked holing up with him. Snuggling in bed together in between their wild sessions of adventuresome lovemaking. She taught Luke everything she knew. And ever the willing pupil, he absorbed everything and gave it right back to her.

They played without any expectation for the future. They made love two or three times a day. Luke making up for lost time, Callie indulging him.

She introduced him to sex toys, body paints and blindfolds. She brought silken cords into the bedroom and they teased each other with light bondage games.

She taught him how to titillate with velvet and feathers and leather. She used lace gloves when she stroked him to orgasm and he returned the favor by rubbing her sensitive cleft with heated massage oils.

They made love in the back of the limo with the privacy window up.

In a hotel in Flagstaff they had an aphrodisiac picnic of oysters and champagne and Turkish delight. They supped on caviar and crackers, cucumbers and hot dogs.

They fed each other from the room service menu. Whipped cream and strawberries. Gooey cheesy pizza that dripped off their chins.

And then they ravished each other for hours.

Luke's technique not only improved but he quickly racked up A plus quality work. When she finished with this guy some lucky woman was going to have the lover of her dreams. Callie congratulated herself on a job well-done and tried not to feel jealous of some fictional woman.

She could hardly believe how far Luke had come in such a short amount of time, dropping his rigid standards, thoughtfully considering other points of view besides his own, relaxing into the ease of an uncommitted relationship. He told her that for the first time in his life he felt as if there were no expectations on him beyond making sure he kept her safe.

His confession was a huge compliment and pleased Callie inordinately.

And while they were exquisitely tender with each other, neither dared murmur words of love.

Good, Callie thought. Good.

This was how it should be. Perfect. In the moment. Now. No worries about tomorrow. No one getting hurt. Just fun.

Who could ask for more?

ON THE EIGHTEENTH DAY of the tour, having just arrived at the Barnes & Noble in Tucson for Callie's 4 p.m. book signing, something happened that changed everything.

Callie was sitting behind a desk at the front of the store surrounded by her fans, Luke stood behind her, silent and watchful. He wore his ubiquitous black suit, black shades and had his hands clasped in front of him.

And he looked incredibly handsome.

She had just autographed a book, *To Jessica, Keep it hot,* and handed it to the shy accountant who'd told Callie her show had given her the courage to sign up for a dating service, when Molly Anne came bouncing over, grinning from ear to ear.

"Could you guys excuse us for a minute?" Molly asked the fans lined up for autographs. "The Midnight Ryder will be right back after a short break."

"What is it?" Callie asked as Molly Anne dragged her off to an alcove, Luke diligently behind them.

"I just got a call from the coordinator of the Jazzy."

"The what?"

"You know, the industry award for the best female personality in radio. Remember, you were nominated for it last month. It's part of the reason we scheduled the West Coast tour when we did, so you could be in L.A. when they handed out the awards."

"Oh yeah. They let you know ahead of time when you win?"

"They just started announcing the winner in advance this year because the nominees were getting so nervous. Last year, the woman from National Public Radio threw up all over the stage."

"That's nice." She hadn't heard Molly Anne. She'd been too busy admiring the way the silky material of Luke's suit skimmed across his butt.

Molly Anne snapped her fingers in Callie's face.

Callie blinked. "Huh."

"You've won the Jazzy!"

She should have been over the moon with excitement. She was not. It was just like when she learned Buck Bryson had been fired and she'd gotten his job. She smiled because that's what Molly Anne seemed to expect.

"We'll be back in L.A. tomorrow. The ceremony is at seven."

"Sounds good," Callie mumbled.

Luke had bent down to pick something up off the floor and she was peering over Molly Anne's shoulder to get a better view.

"Dammit, Callie, will you stop thinking about screwing that man for two seconds? You just won one of the top awards in the business. It's like winning the freaking Golden Globe. Be excited about it for me if not for yourself."

That got her attention. Molly Anne rarely spoke so frankly. Or so crudely. Shock talk was Callie's bailiwick.

"I won the award, Molly Anne. Not you. Get over yourself."

Molly Anne's face shattered. She spun on her heel and fled around the next row of bookshelves.

The minute the words were out of her mouth, Callie felt horrible.

"That was harsh," Luke said.

It was harsh. Unnecessarily so. Contrition and regret punched her hard in the chest.

"Molly Anne, wait." Callie turned and hurried after her friend.

She found her in the children's section, perched on

a tiny chair, flipping through the pages of *Goodnight Moon*. She had her glasses pushed up on top of her head and tears were sliding slowly down her cheeks.

Callie pulled up a tot-size stool and plunked down beside her. She laid a hand on Molly Anne's shoulder. "I'm sorry. That was uncalled for. I've just been very… um, distracted lately."

Molly Anne swiped at her eyes with the knuckles of her index fingers. "It's Luke. You've replaced me with him. You used to tell me everything, Callie. Now you tell it to him instead."

So Molly Anne was jealous of the attention she'd been giving to Luke. At least that explained her emotional outburst.

Callie slung an arm over her shoulder, drew her close to comfort her. "Don't be jealous of Luke, Moll. You know he's temporary. He's just a guy. He'll be gone when the tour is over."

Molly Anne did not look appeased. "He's different."

"How so?"

"You really care for this one."

Callie's face curled into a no-way-Jose expression, but her heart sped up. Did she feel differently about Luke?

"No I don't," she denied, as much to herself as to Molly Anne.

"You do. I can tell by the way you look at him." Molly Anne flipped another page of *Goodnight Moon* and did not meet Callie's gaze.

"Hey, remember the pact we made when we were sixteen?"

Molly Anne shrugged.

Callie cupped her friend's chin and forced her to stare her in the eye. "What was our pact?"

"Men will come and men will go but we'll be friends forever."

"Right."

"Are you seriously telling me Luke doesn't mean anything to you?" Molly Anne asked.

"Oh, honey," Callie said, injecting her voice with the full affect of her Midnight Ryder Southern drawl, trying to cheer Molly Anne up and make her laugh. "That man means nothing more to me that a high-quality vibrator."

Molly Anne smiled then and Callie plucked a clean tissue from her pocket and passed it over so she could dry her tears. Mission accomplished. All was forgiven between them.

"I guess we better get back to work." Molly Anne laughed shakily and dabbed at her eyes. "You've got books to sign and I've got a victory party to plan. I'm thinking of giving Brooke Burnett a call, see if the *Celebrity Insider* would be willing to send a crew to film you accepting the Jazzy."

"You do that." Callie nodded and stood up to return to the book-signing table. That's when she saw Luke standing at the end of the aisle and realized he must have heard every stupid word she'd just uttered.

14

THE TELEPHONE in Callie's hotel room rang at ten-thirty-five that night, just a few minutes after Brooke Burnett announced on *Celebrity Insider* that the smokin' hot Callie Ryder would be accepting her first Jazzy in L.A. on Saturday evening during a banquet at the Beverly Hills Grand Hotel.

Luke and Callie had never talked about what he might have overheard in the bookstore. She didn't know how to broach the subject and he never brought it up. In fact, he acted no differently toward her and she began to think that maybe he hadn't heard the vibrator comment.

He was in the shower and Callie was in a terry-cloth bathrobe blowing her hair dry in front of the dressing-table mirror after a particularly messy and very arousing game of *Chocolate, chocolate, who's got the chocolate,* grew way out of hand.

She'd been admiring her hair color and thinking she might stick with her natural shade. She'd been changing the color every few months since becoming the Midnight Ryder, but there was nothing wrong with basic honey brown for a while.

The phone rang again.

Callie switched off the blow-dryer and got up to walk across the room to answer it, figuring it was probably her mother calling to congratulate her on the Jazzy or Molly Anne with yet another endless to-do list to go over with Callie before tomorrow's jam-packed schedule began.

"'Lo," she said, tilting her head to tuck the receiver between her chin and shoulder.

She reached for the hand lotion beside the sink, squirted some into her palms while she cocked one leg in the chair she'd vacated. She started to slather the milky scented lotion on her shins when the voice on the other end of the line stopped her in midmotion.

"This time I won't miss like I did outside the bar in Los Angeles," came the whispered, gravelly sound of her stalker.

Fear slithered down Callie's spine, but her anger was stronger than her fear. "You tried to run me down, you jerk."

"No. It was a warning. Which you didn't heed. If I had wanted to run you down, trust me, you would have been dead."

"I'm not scared of you," Callie said through gritted teeth, her fist wrapped tightly around the receiver.

"You better be scared of me because I'm deadly serious."

Before she had time to tell the guy to stick his death threats, Luke shot from the bathroom like a bullet from a gun, a skimpy white towel wrapped around his waist, fury on his face.

"Is it him?" he asked, snatching the phone from her hand. "The stalker?"

Dumbfounded by his swift response, Callie nodded. Clearly, he'd been waiting for this moment ever since the guy had tried to run her down.

"Listen here," Luke growled, but even from where she was standing, Callie could hear the dial tone as the creep hung up.

Luke turned to her. "Next time you get him on the line, call me immediately. You could have strung him along while I called the police on my cell and had them trace the call."

"Sorry. I just got so mad, I didn't think."

He reached for her and in the process let go of his towel. She fell against that big strong chest, nestled her head there. His arms went tight around her. She felt so safe in his embrace.

Pressing his lips against her temple, he kissed her then murmured, "Word by word, Callie, tell me everything that bastard said."

And so she told him. As he held her and kissed her and gently stroked her body.

Molly Anne was right. Luke was different from other men.

He was changing her. Sex with him was changing her. Their games, the role-playing stretched the boundaries of their identity, altering their perceptions of each other.

This man was taking her places she had never been before, carrying her into a safe harbor she'd only dreamed of. A calm, balmy place where she felt cocooned, protected and tenderly cared for.

And she was terrified she was getting too accustomed to it. This feeling of safety. What in the world would she do when it was gone?

When he was no longer in her life?

They only had three more days together. The realization made her sad. Callie gulped. Could she be falling in love with him?

Impossible.

Unbelievable.

She barely knew him and yet whenever he touched her or smiled at her, a poignancy so sharp and sweet shot through her that it made her heart ache.

It's because he's your fantasy man. He's fulfilled your long-held secret and now you have nothing to replace it with. That's the problem. That's what's wrong.

She wasn't falling in love. Love was for fools. How many times had Momma told her that?

Okay, so she wasn't in love with him. But she wanted him. Badly.

"Make love to me," she whispered. And she meant make love, not have sex. "I need to feel you inside me."

"You don't have to ask twice, sweetheart."

He lifted her in his arms and carried her to bed. He seemed to know exactly what she needed. He'd become that attuned to her. Nothing rushed, nothing desperate, not even anything playful. He made love to her slow, soft and tender.

His lips carried her away. His hands cherished her with caresses. Callie let herself drift, consumed by the sweet, sadness of it all.

Nothing mattered except the moment. Not the past. Not the future. Only now.

After a long while Luke shifted, going from long, tender thrusts to short, quicker ones.

"Yes," she whimpered, her eyes squeezed tightly shut. "I like that. More. Deeper. Harder. I want you to fill me up. Please, more…give me more."

She tightened around him with each thrust and parry. Her heart pounded in her chest, in her ears, in her head, swamping her body with a heat so intense she felt as if she were literally on fire with him. For him.

He stopped moving and stared into her face. "Callie," he whispered.

"What's wrong?"

"Look at me."

She raised her lashes to peer up at him and she almost stopped breathing at the look of longing in his eyes.

With his gaze fastened on her, Luke began to move again.

He filled her, wholly, completely. She had never experienced anything like the perfect union she felt with him.

It wasn't his masculine power—although he certainly was strong and manly. It wasn't simply an estrogen dump. It wasn't the inexperienced lover aspect, for he'd already far surpassed novice level. It wasn't even that they didn't have much time left.

Rather it was the yearning in his eyes. The solid link between them. The sensation that they were the only two people in the world.

It was all too much emotion. Too much to contemplate.

She broke her visual bond with him. Closing her eyes, shutting herself off, pulling away, shutting down these feelings.

Luke thrust harder, faster. Callie mewled her pleasure. She ran her nails down his back, scratching him
lightly. She wrapped her legs around his waist and clung
tight. She lifted her head off the pillow and nibbled on
his bottom lip.

"Almost," she cried. "Don't stop."

He pushed into her one last time, and Callie con-
vulsed around him at the same time his masculine essence shot from his body filling the condom he'd put on
during their foreplay.

And that's when Callie realized her period was four
days late.

"I WANT YOU TO DO something for me, Callie," Luke said
as they lay curled against each other, luxuriating in the
afterglow of sex. She looked up at him; her sweet, petite
body felt so solidly wonderful in his arms it literally hurt
his heart. "Promise me you'll give it some consideration."

"What is it?"

"Don't go to the banquet. Cancel the last couple of
days of the tour. Go back home to New York."

The expression on her face and the way she was slowly
shaking her head told him that she wasn't going to agree.
Not even for him. But what else had he expected? One
of the things he cherished most about Callie was her
courage. Yet he couldn't shake the mournful feeling deep
inside him that something bad was going to happen.

"Luke, I can't let this jackal terrorize me."

"What if I can't protect you?" he asked. "What if I
can't keep you safe?"

"I have complete faith in you." She leaned against

him, lightly running her tongue along his chin. "Besides, I have the mace you gave me."

He knew what she was doing. She'd done it before. In fact, that was how he'd ended up breaking his code of ethics and taking her to bed in the first place.

"You're using sex to block your feelings," he said, sharing with her what he'd observed about her behavior. He doubted she was even aware of it herself.

"What are you talking about?"

"You're scared as hell but too brave to show it. You want to quit but you're too proud to admit it."

"Rather a case of the pot calling the kettle black, don't you think."

"No. I don't use sex as a way to sublimate my fear," he said.

"Neither do I."

"Then prove it to me, just don't go to the banquet."

"I can't do that."

"I might not be able to save your life, Callie." Luke's voice cracked under the strain of trying to convince her to see things his way. "Can't you understand? I'm just one man."

"But a very potent one." Her fingertips grazed his half-hard cock.

"Stop that, please. Sex isn't going to solve this."

"No, but it might make you less testy."

"Good grief, woman, we just made love for an hour. Don't you ever get enough?" He hadn't meant to sound so harsh, he'd simply wanted to get her attention and make her listen to his concerns.

She licked her lips. "Of you? Never."

He pulled back. He was beginning to feel like a side of beef. "Don't give me that. You could easily replace me with a high-quality vibrator."

It had never been his intention to bring up that casual offhand comment he'd heard her make to Molly Anne. It had hurt but he'd never let on.

If he was falling in love with her, it was his own damn fault. But no matter how much he tried to steel himself against the vibrator remark, it still cut him. He was nothing more to her than a walking, talking sex toy. He'd known that from the beginning. She'd never deceived him about her intentions.

"Luke, I'm sorry about that crack. I was just trying to cheer Molly Anne up."

"By putting me down?"

"No, I…" She reached for him but he shrugged her hand away. "I'm so sorry. I never meant to hurt you."

"I can handle it. Hey, if the truth hurts, wear it, right? I don't shy from the reality. You never said it would be different. The mistake was all mine."

For some reason that remark cut her to the bone. Luke didn't know why, but he saw it register in her face, caught the haunted vulnerability in her eyes. That flash of uncertainty said she was trying desperately to hide something important from herself.

Or from him.

"Come on," she dared, rolling away from him and sitting up against the headboard. "Express your anger. Give me what for. Let me have it. I deserve the full brunt of your temper. Dammit, let go of control for once in your life, Cardasian."

"I can't let go, Callie. Not again. I already let go with you once and damned if it isn't proving my undoing."

"What do you mean?" She lifted her chin, readying herself for conflict.

He realized she'd done it again. She found a way to hide her doubts about her motives. Her subconscious probably figured if she couldn't seduce him, then she would provoke him. She would use any defense mechanism in her arsenal to keep from examining her own fears.

"What I meant," he said, looking her dead in the eyes. "Is that you're too much woman for a simple guy like me."

NERVOUSNESS BIT INTO HIM sharp as a New York winter wind. Luke hovered in the wings offstage watching Molly Anne fiddle with Callie's corsage as she prepared her to walk up to the podium and accept the Jazzy.

Luke spoke softly into the tiny microphone in his two-way headphone radio and asked Zack, "How's the crowd looking from your angle?"

The room was packed with over a hundred people, savoring the crêpes Suzette that capped off a meal of prime rib as the program started.

Waiters zigzagged between the round tables, carting giant platters of empty dishes back to the kitchen. Others were winding from guest to guest offering coffee to go with dessert.

Last night when Callie had refused to cancel her appearance at the awards banquet in spite of the stalker's continued threats, he had called for reinforcements. Not only had he flown Zack in, but Luke had also updated the LAPD on what had transpired since they'd filed the near hit-and-run report.

Right now three uniformed police officers manned the exits. If the stalker was in the ballroom and he dared make a move on Callie, he wasn't getting out those doors without being apprehended.

Zack was positioned in the audience along with several members of the Beverly Hills Grand Hotel's security staff, at the ready for the first sign of trouble.

"So far so good, bro," Zack said. "Let's hope her stalker is full of idle threats."

"Stay alert," Luke radioed back.

"Always. Over and out, dude."

Luke took another quick look backstage, making sure no one was hiding in the shadows. Quickly, he returned his attention to the ceremony.

From where he stood, if he craned his neck, he could see Brooke Burnett and her camera crew filming the proceedings. Molly Anne Armstrong was some kind of dynamo when it came to promoting Callie's career. Her devotion to her friend was truly remarkable.

They called Callie's name.

She climbed three steps up to the dais, the overhead spotlight following her progress. She sauntered her hips in that provocative Southern way of hers on heels too high. But she never once teetered.

She was that damned self-assured.

God, but she looked breathtaking in the little black dress that lovingly hugged her curves. It occurred to Luke that this was the first time he had ever seen her wearing something classic and tailored. With the focus off her outlandish clothes and funny-colored hair, she looked absolutely stunning.

Who would have thought that antagonistic little shock jock in combat boots and purple hair could clean up so nice? But inside this polished, professional exterior—that was probably all Molly Anne's doing in the first place—Luke knew, lurked the soul of a true rebel. Not many like her in the world and that was the person he really loved. The real Callie.

Not the Midnight Ryder. Not the polished persona she was presenting now, but the inner woman he'd come to know intimately over the past nineteen days.

Sweet yet saucy. Brave and yet vulnerable. Tender and tough and spontaneous and sexy as any woman walking the planet.

Callie Ryder was one of a kind. His gut clenched, along with his heart.

She was the most amazing person he had ever known. She didn't give two figs for what people thought of her. And even though she was small of stature, in personality she was larger than life. Much larger than he and his constricted views. She had expanded his world. Expanded his mind. Expanded his heart.

And he was going to miss her with every bone in his body.

Focus on the job, Cardasian. You're here for a reason. Her life is in your hands. You can't afford to get sidetracked. You screw up. She could die.

The presenter bestowed her with the golden statue and then stepped aside for Callie to give her acceptance speech.

Callie adjusted the microphone to her height. She made a couple of mildly off-color jokes that had the crowd rolling with laughter. She thanked her mother, her family at KSXX, her dear friend and business manager, Molly Anne Armstrong.

And then, just when he thought she was finished, Callie cleared her throat. "There's someone else I must thank. I haven't known him very long, but he has affected my life in so many ways I don't know where to start."

Was she talking about him? What was she going to say? Was this her goodbye speech to him?

He didn't want to hear it. Not here. Not like this. Not in front of all these people.

Hell, he didn't want to say goodbye at all. He had violated his most basic values and he'd gotten hurt. He had known better, but he had succumbed to temptation. He'd allowed himself to be seduced by the idea of no-strings-attached sex and now he was all tied up in knots. There was nothing to do but live with the painful consequences.

"He's taught me so much," Callie said. "About honor and integrity and sticking by your word. And because of him I have a very special announcement to make. But let me tell you a little bit about Luke. First, he's my bodyguard."

A titter of surprise ran through the crowd. Luke tensed.

"What's going on?" Zack's voice crackled over the radio. "Is she about to out the stalker?"

Knowing his stubborn, brave Callie the way he did, Luke realized that must be what she was planning.

Whether the daring tactic was right or wrong, he had to give her credit at the same time he wanted to shake some sense into her. The woman had more chutzpah in her little finger than most men did in their entire bodies.

"I've been receiving death threats because of my outspoken views on sex. In fact, the cowardly stalker called me last night. He told me not to accept this award. He told me to turn down my new time slot on KSXX, quit my job or he would kill me."

The crowd gasped and turned in their chairs to glance nervously around the room.

"Well," Callie said and blew a raspberry into the mike. "That's what I think of men who try to terrorize women into behaving the way they want them to behave."

"Oh shit!" Zack's voice exploded in Luke's ear.

"What is it, what is it?" Luke cried.

He was on the move, shoving aside the stage curtain, scanning the audience for what Zack was seeing.

"Waiter with a gun!"

The crowd must have spotted the gun-toting waiter at the same moment Zack did. Collectively, people jumped to their feet, knocking over tables, banging into each other, running for the exits.

Women shrieked. Men shouted. Glass shattered.

Brooke Burnett's camera crew was filming madly as the drama unfolded while Brooke took cover behind a burly security guard.

Luke's eyes finally found the waiter amidst the melee.

There. At the apron of the stage, waving a .45 caliber handgun. He was a balding middle-aged man with long hair, red-faced and yelling, calling Callie every vicious, ugly name in the book.

Callie calmly held her ground, staring the guy down as if she didn't have a lick of sense in her head.

"Dive down behind the podium, Callie," Luke yelled but she either didn't hear him in the chaos or chose to disobey him. Again.

From the back of the room, Luke saw his brother come charging over tables and around guests to get to the waiter in time to prevent certain catastrophe.

But Zack was too far away.

If the waiter got a head shot off, Callie would be killed instantly.

Without a single thought for his own life, Luke hurtled himself from the stage. And leaped onto the waiter.

Just as the gun went off.

15

"LUKE!" CALLIE SCREAMED.

She had to get to him. She flung down the golden statue she'd just won. It hit the stage with a crack and split into two pieces. Callie barely noticed, didn't even care. Only one thought dominated her mind.

Luke.

She vaulted over the Jazzy presenter who was trembling in a ball underneath the podium steps. She came down hard and the heel of one shoe broke off.

Luke.

She stumbled, hesitated long enough to rip off her shoes, then kept going. She was too short to see him above the mob.

Was he hurt? Was he dead?

No. God, please no. Let him be okay. He had to be okay. She had so much to tell him. Things she should have told him last night. But she'd wanted to wait and do it at the banquet. On camera. In front of witnesses so there would be no chance of letting fear change her mind.

"Let me through," she insisted, pushing people aside as she struggled to get to him.

In the distance she heard the scream of sirens. More

police backups? Or was it an ambulance siren? She spied Zack in the crowd, a look of shocked disbelief on his face. Cops, guns drawn, had surrounded Callie's assailant.

But Luke? Where was Luke? She couldn't see him.

Finally, finally, she found a hole through the crowd and came nose to button with a burly policeman. "My bodyguard," she cried. "Where's my bodyguard?"

"We need for you to stay back, ma'am." The policeman put up a palm.

"But my bodyguard," She was jacking herself up on her tiptoes, trying uselessly to see around the six-foot cop. "He put his life on the line for me." She gestured to where Luke had to be lying on the ground just a few feet behind all those policemen.

"That's what bodyguards do, ma'am, it's their job."

You don't understand, Callie wanted to sob. My bodyguard is different. He's so much more than my protector. He's also my lover and my best friend.

She *was* in love.

The realization hit her like a blast of hot air from a stoked furnace.

She loved him.

And not just because he'd saved her life. A piece of her had started falling in love with him the night he walked into the radio station, so big and commanding and in control.

Her Sir Galahad.

He was everything she'd ever wanted. Everything she had ever needed. She had just been too afraid to face it.

"Just tell me if he's all right. Just tell me if he's hurt."

Callie gulped and wrung her hands. "Tell me if he's alive."

"No one got killed, ma'am."

At that moment, one of the officers pulled a man to his feet. Her assailant. In spite of the cuts and bruises on his face, Callie immediately recognized the handcuffed man. How could she not recognize him? Night after night she'd stared at his poster on the walls at KSXX.

"Bitch," Buck Bryson snarled when he spotted her. "You stole my time slot. You took my job! I warned you to quit. I told you to stop your tour, but no, you wouldn't back off. Pushing, always pushing people to their limits. You drove me to this. It's all your fault."

Callie stared, openmouthed as the police led him away. Chills ran up her arms.

She heard Brooke Burnett's excited voice in the background as her camera crew apparently caught Bryson's rant but Callie didn't care.

She was sorry about Bryson. Remorseful she'd been the catalyst that had caused him to snap, but she had no time for regrets. She had to find Luke.

The place was in utter disarray. Personal belongings strewn across the ballroom, the police methodically gathering evidence, herding people aside so they could record their statements, while hotel personnel tried to smooth ruffled feathers.

Callie felt a hand at her elbow and her heart leaped. She turned. It wasn't Luke at her side, but Molly Anne.

"Are you all right?" she asked, clutching her chest. "When Buck Bryson started waving that gun at you I thought I was going to die on the spot."

"Oh, Molly Anne." Callie embraced her. Until she saw her friend's concerned face, she hadn't realized how shaken up she was.

"I can't believe Buck is the one who has been stalking you," Molly Anne said. "He must have been incredibly jealous to have done such a thing."

"Where's Luke?" Callie asked her. "Have you seen Luke?"

Molly Anne frowned. "Not since he jumped Buck."

"He has to be here. Where is he?"

"Shh." Molly Anne patted her back. "You're getting yourself all worked up."

Molly Anne was right. She was getting worked up. But she had to see Luke. She had so much to tell him.

Where was he? He was tall. He should stand out. She should be able to see him.

She scanned the crowd but she must have moved her head too quickly because the room spun and she suddenly felt sick to her stomach. Swallowing hard, she fought off the nausea.

"You don't look so good," Molly Anne said. "Let's go up to your hotel room. You can lie down, while I come back and look for Luke."

"No." She didn't want to leave the ballroom. "The police will want to talk to me and I can't leave without seeing Luke. I…"

Another wave of dizziness hit and this time Callie knew there was no fighting it. She was going to throw up.

LUKE SAT IN the manager's office of the Beverly Hills Grand Hotel, surrounded by the head of security, two uniformed police officers and the new guy who'd just arrived. The officer in charge.

After Luke had flattened Buck Bryson in the ballroom, the two cops had pulled him off the guy and whisked him into this office.

Luke didn't even remember. But his knuckles were skinned and bruised, so he must have given the guy a beating. Nobody threatened his Callie and got away with it.

They'd kept him waiting an hour before they had even taken his statement and he was getting antsy. Something weird was going on and he wanted to know what it was. He was anxious to get out of here and find Callie.

"Have you talked to Ms. Ryder?" he asked for the thirteenth time since they'd hauled him in here and told him to wait. "Is she all right?"

"She's resting comfortably in her room. One of my men is upstairs taking her statement now," the officer in charge reassured him. His name badge identified him as Lieutenant James Smothers.

But Luke wasn't reassured. He had to see her for himself.

"Bryson wants to press charges against you, for assault with a deadly weapon," Smothers said.

"On what grounds? I was just doing my job."

"You beat him up pretty badly. You're a big man. Young. Strong."

"He was attempting to take my client's life," Luke said.

"Not with this he wasn't." From his jacket pocket, Smothers took what looked to be the .45 Bryson had been waving at Callie and tossed it on the table in front of him.

Luke picked up the gun, studied it a moment, then looked up at Smothers in confusion. "It's a toy?"

"Movie prop gun actually."

"But there was gunfire. Everyone heard it."

"Blanks."

Luke blew out his breath and dropped his forehead into his open palm. "But why?"

"Bryson is saying he just wanted to scare Ms. Ryder into resigning from KSXX. He was desperate to get his job back."

Luke lifted his head, met Smothers' gaze. "But he tried to run Callie over with his car in Los Angeles."

"According to Bryson, that wasn't him."

"And you believe him?"

"He admits he was watching Ms. Ryder, following her. He saw a drunk swerve and almost hit her, saw you push her out of the way in the nick of time. He used the opportunity to his advantage. Bryson called her and claimed he was driving the car and warned her off. He admits all that."

"He's a liar."

Smothers shrugged. "There's something else."

"What?"

"Bryson wants to talk to you."

"He'll have to wait," Luke said, pushing up from the table. "I have to see Callie first."

CALLIE LAY ON THE BED in her hotel room. Her head had finally stopped spinning and her stomach had quieted, but she was still afraid to sit up and test her equilibrium. She wasn't in any rush to start upchucking again.

She gazed at the ceiling, thinking about what had just happened, thinking about Luke, wondering what was taking Molly Anne so long to locate him.

She had so much to tell him. Especially since she hadn't gotten to make the announcement she'd intended to make, thanks to Buck Bryson's interruption.

She'd been planning to announce her resignation from KSXX. Because she had come to realize she did not want to be the Midnight Ryder anymore. She had done everything she had set out to do. She'd risen to the top of the radio business. She'd achieved a top industry award. She'd helped a lot of young women find their self-esteem.

But now it was time to help herself. Figure out what she wanted to do with the rest of her life.

And her decision had nothing to do with Buck Bryson and his threats and everything to do with the fact her period was five days late.

And she'd never been late.

Well, except for that one time. When she was sixteen and certain she was pregnant with Chip's baby.

Callie could still remember the smell of the clinic, all antiseptic and serious business. When she closed her eyes she could see the nurses with their sad but understanding eyes. She could taste her own fear, hot on the back of her tongue.

Molly Anne had gone with her to the clinic because Chip had flaked out, broken up with her. Just like a man, her mother would have said if she had known about it.

Callie could have told her mother about the pregnancy, but even a girl with a forward-thinking mom, still wanted to keep some things private. So it had been Molly Anne holding her hand and sitting with her on that hard vinyl bench.

With vivid clarity, she recalled the abject relief when the nurse had come back to tell her the pregnancy test was negative. She didn't have to make a decision about having an abortion.

And from that day forward, Callie had always used two methods of birth control. The pill and condoms.

Except for the first night she and Luke had made love.

And now she was five days late.

There was a home pregnancy test kit in her purse. She'd bought it that morning. She'd almost taken it but had decided to wait until after the banquet, after she'd made her announcement. Until she and Luke were alone together.

She was terrified. Scared to death.

Was she pregnant with Luke's baby?

"Let her sleep, Luke. She's exhausted."

"I need to see her." He was standing outside Callie's hotel room, Molly Anne blocking his way. His belongings were in the hallway at her feet.

"What's this?" he asked.

"Your things."

"I can see that. Why are they out here?"

"The tour is over. There's no reason for you to hang around. Go back to New York. Go back to your life."

"Not without seeing Callie first."

"She's sick."

"I just want to say goodbye."

"And what? You want to tell her you've fallen in love with her?"

"How do you know that?"

"I've seen the way you look at her. But believe me, she doesn't feel the same way about you. Don't embarrass yourself. Don't make her have to break your heart to your face."

He clenched his jaw, fisted his hands. Molly Anne had a point but he still had to tell Callie how he felt, even if he did end up getting hurt big-time.

"I need to see her."

"She's just not the forever kind, Luke. Callie belongs to the public. She's a star. And even if she did have feelings for you, how could you take her away from all that?"

"I wouldn't want her to stop doing what she loves, but I have to tell her how I feel."

"If you really love her, Luke, then you'll do what's best for her. You'll go away and leave her alone."

"WHERE'S LUKE?" Callie asked sleepily when Molly Anne came back into the hotel room. She must have dozed off. She felt pretty woozy after drinking some hot tea Molly Anne had ordered for her from room service to settle her stomach. She almost felt as if she'd been drugged with Valium.

"He's gone back to New York."

"What?" Callie came up off the bed too fast and her head spun. She had to sit on the edge a moment and let her mind clear. "Why did Luke leave?"

Molly Anne shrugged. "Bryson's behind bars. I canceled the last two book signings. His job was over."

"He left without saying goodbye?"

Molly nodded. "Men. Your Momma is right. Harleys, the lot of them."

"That doesn't make any sense. His things are all still…" Callie looked around the room and saw that Luke's things were gone.

"He asked me to pack them up while you were sleeping. He didn't want to wake you. He thought it would be easier this way."

But that made no sense. Callie blinked. Her head felt stuffed with cotton. She was having a hard time thinking. "This is awful."

"Honey, he's just a man, another will be along shortly," Molly Anne soothed.

"No. You don't understand. I think I might be pregnant," Callie confessed.

"What?" Molly Anne stared at her as if she'd just announced she was having a sex-change operation.

Callie nodded.

"It's Luke's?"

"Of course."

"How could this happen? Aren't you on the pill?"

"I accidentally skipped one."

"How could you forget to take a pill?" Molly Anne shouted. "God, Callie, didn't that scare in high school teach you anything?"

"The tour was hectic. I just forgot. It was only one time. Besides, you're not my mother. I won't ask you to baby-sit. Don't come unhinged."

"But you're the Midnight Ryder. You can't be pregnant. This is going to be a publicity nightmare," Molly Anne ranted. "The hippest sex guru in the country, the one woman who is supposed to know how to take care of herself in bed gets knocked up. Lovely. The show will be ruined."

Callie cleared her throat. Now obviously wasn't the time to break the news that she was quitting the show anyway. Even if she wasn't pregnant. She'd had enough.

"Don't you think you're overreacting? We don't even know for sure that I am pregnant. But I've got a home pregnancy kit in my purse."

Molly Anne brightened at that. "Well what are you waiting for? Get in the bathroom and pee on that stick. Let's find out if we have something to freak out about or not."

"I wanted to wait for Luke," Callie said and to her shock, her bottom lip started trembling.

"Well, he ain't coming, honey. He took a hike on you, just like Chip did."

"But he didn't know I might be pregnant. I have to tell him."

"Take the test. Find out first."

Callie got the kit from her purse and went into the bathroom. "Start timing," she called to Molly Anne through the door. "Sixty seconds."

Molly Anne came into the bathroom where Callie was standing at the sink, staring at the plastic dip stick. "Thirty seconds," she said.

"Read the box to me again. Which is which?"

"If one line turns pink it's negative. If two turn it's positive."

Callie held her breath. One of the lines had started to turn.

"Forty-five seconds," Molly Anne said. "Fifty. Fifty-five. That's it. Sixty seconds. What's it say?"

Callie looked down at the stick and promptly burst into tears.

16

"I DIDN'T WRITE those letters," Buck Bryson told Luke the next morning from his prison cell in the L.A. county jail.

"No? Then who did?"

"I don't know."

"Why should I believe you?"

"Because a real crazy is still out there after her."

"And you're not the real crazy?"

"What I did was wrong, desperate. I know that now." Buck pushed a long strand of wispy gray hair behind an ear. "But I never intended on hurting Callie. I just wanted to scare her. Get her to quit so I could have my job back. I knew I was in trouble. There'd been warnings. My ratings were slipping. Callie's star was rising."

"Yeah, yeah, get to the point."

"I hadn't even planned on threatening her until I heard about the letters. I thought, hey, I could escalate the whole thing by calling her and people would think it was the guy who'd been writing the letters. But it got out of control. I never meant it to deteriorate the way it did and that's why I had to talk to you. There's someone out there who means Callie real harm."

"How did you find out about the letters?" Luke asked.

"Molly Anne."

That gave him pause. Bryson might be lying or crazy or both but no harm would come by checking out his story. As he left the jail, he placed a call to Zack.

"Hey, I got an assignment for you."

"What's up?"

"Run a background check on Molly Anne Armstrong for me, will you? Something's not right."

"WHY ARE YOU STILL CRYING?" Molly Anne asked. "It's been two days. The test was negative. You're not pregnant. Now our lives can go on as before. You and me. Together. Forever."

Callie wiped away the tears trickling down her face. Silly, she knew, mourning for a child that had never been. Until the moment when she'd looked down and seen one solitary pink line she had no idea how much she'd wanted to be pregnant. But her emotions told her two very important things.

One, quitting the shock jock business was definitely what she wanted and two, she had to find Luke and tell him exactly how much she loved him.

"Molly Anne," Callie said. "There's something I must tell you."

"Well, as long as you're not pregnant, I don't care what it is." Molly Anne was busy packing their suitcases. Their flight back to New York left in two hours.

"I'm quitting KSXX."

"What?"

"Yes. I've been thinking about it for a while. Long before this tour actually. I just didn't realize how unhappy I was until I met Luke."

"You're talking crazy," Molly Anne said. "You've made it. You're at the pinnacle of your career. Why would you want to quit now?"

"Because I am at the pinnacle of my career and I know I don't want to be fifty years old and still running around trying to shock people. It's okay for a rebellious teen or a young twenty-something looking to find herself, but I'll be twenty-nine next month and I'm ready for a new chapter."

"You can't do this." Molly Anne's nostrils flared.

"I know you're upset but you'll find another job. I'm sure you can even stay at KSXX."

"But I don't want to stay there without you. We're a team, you and me. Molly Anne and Callie together forever. Just like in our pact. We signed it in blood, remember?" Molly Anne's eyes were wild.

"We were kids."

"I've taken care of you all these years. I've been behind the scenes pushing and pushing and pushing and now you're just going to toss me aside." Molly Anne splayed an irate palm against her chest. "And for what, some…some…man?"

"Did you drug my tea yesterday? Is that why I feel so groggy?"

"It was for your own good. I had to keep you knocked out so I could get rid of Luke."

"You're losing it," Callie said and moved to shoulder past her.

"No!" Molly Anne screamed. "This is simply unacceptable. I love you, dammit. I've been here for you. I won't let you throw me over like this."

That's when Molly Anne pulled the gun from her pocket, and she clearly had no idea how to use the weapon because she waved it wildly around, pointing it first at Callie, then pressing it to her own temple as she sobbed.

Callie had to disarm her before she killed one or both of them. "Take it easy."

"Don't tell me to take it easy."

Think, think. She had to get out of this. Slowly, Callie reached for her purse on the bedside table.

Molly Anne caught her movements and swung the gun at her. "Stay still."

"I'm just going for some lipstick," Callie said, trying to sound offhand, her heart thumping erratically.

"What do you need lipstick for? *Luke* isn't coming to see you."

"My lips are dry, okay? I've been doing a lot of crying."

Molly Anne nodded and lowered the gun just a fraction. Callie opened her purse and fumbled for the lipstick.

She eased it out and before Molly Anne knew what hit her, Callie maced her.

Molly Anne howled.

Callie tackled her.

The gun flew from Molly Anne's grasp. Callie landed heavily on her old friend.

Molly Anne scratched at Callie's eyes. Callie raised an arm to block the assault. Molly Anne used that brief hesitation to squirm away. Blinking and brawling, she crawled for the gun.

"Callie!" Luke's voice ripped through the hotel room

and in a second he and Zack and hotel security were standing there looking down at them.

Callie had never seen a more beautiful sight.

"MOLLY ANNE WAS THE ONE who wrote those threatening letters," Luke explained. Zack had departed, too, leaving them to their privacy. "After Buck told me he didn't write the letters I asked Zack to contact Roger and the NYPD with my suspicions about Molly Anne. I was just terrified I wasn't going to get here in time before she cracked."

"But why would she do that?" Callie asked, puzzled. "Why would Molly Anne want to harm me?"

"It was all a publicity stunt. She was so desperate for you to get Bryson's slot that she thought creating a threat would boost your ratings enough to give you that extra push to send you to the top."

"She's always been a master at publicity and the real drive behind my career," Callie admitted.

"Molly Anne didn't have the personality for the success she craved, so she lived vicariously through you. Your success was her success."

"That's why she freaked out so much when I said I wanted to quit KSXX. I guess in her own twisted way she did care deeply for me."

"Love can do strange things to people," he said. "Make them behave in ways they ordinarily never would have."

"But why did she send those threatening letters to the station? It was almost like she wanted me to quit."

"Not at all. That was designed to stir controversy in your show, boost the ratings. Remember that guy that called the night I showed up in the studio?"

"Dave from Albany? How could I forget? We had our first fight because of him." She grinned.

"With the help of the NYPD Roger found out Molly Anne was the one who hired him to threaten you on the air."

Callie shook her head. "It's a lot to absorb. You'd think you know a person after eighteen years."

"Some people you can be acquainted with a lifetime and still never know them," he said softly. "Others, you know them to their soul the minute you meet them."

"Is that right?" She tipped her head back, studying him from beneath her eyelashes.

"Yep."

"And which category do I fall into?"

"I know you don't really have to ask," he said, pulling her tight against his chest and forcing her to look at him straight on.

"Oh my," she whispered.

"And I will go on knowing you into infinity. The reason things didn't work out for us with other people was because we were meant for each other Callie Ryder."

"You mean you're not a Harley?"

He frowned. "I don't get it."

She waved a hand. "I'll tell you some other time. It's a theory of my mother's. Basically, she thinks all men will do you wrong, given the chance. I guess I absorbed a lot of her prejudices."

"But you knew I was different from the start, didn't you?"

"Look at the ego on you. How do I know you're different?"

Luke pinned her legs between his, pressed his lips to her ears and whispered, "Because sweetheart, you don't hear my feet running."

And she knew then, it was true. With this man, she had nothing to fear. Nothing to fight. Nothing to prove.

At long last, she could be her true self.

And it felt glorious.

HARLEQUIN® *Blaze*™

Get ready to check in to Hush...

Piper Devon has opened a hot new hotel
that caters to the senses...and it's giving
ex-lover Trace Winslow a few sleepless nights.

Check out
#178 HUSH
by Jo Leigh
Available April 2005

Book #1, Do Not Disturb miniseries

Look for linked stories by Isabel Sharpe,
Alison Kent, Nancy Warren, Debbi Rawlins
and Jill Shalvis in the months to come!

Shhh...Do Not Disturb

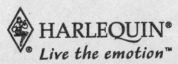

HARLEQUIN®
Live the emotion™

THE CRENSHAWS OF TEXAS

**Brothers bound by blood
and the land they call home!**

DOUBLE IDENTITY

(Silhouette Desire #1646,
available April 2005)

by Annette Broadrick

Undercover agent Jude Crenshaw
had only gotten involved with
Carina Patterson for the sake of
cracking a smuggling case against
her brothers. But close quarters soon
led to a shared attraction, and Jude
could only hope his double identity
wouldn't break both their hearts.

*Available at your
favorite retail outlet.*

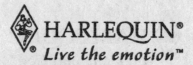

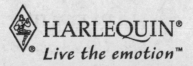